I0648619

Fire Dept. of San Francisco

Report of the Board of Fire Commissioners

Chief Engineer and Fire Alarm Superintendent of the San Francisco Fire

Department

Fire Dept. of San Francisco

Report of the Board of Fire Commissioners
Chief Engineer and Fire Alarm Superintendent of the San Francisco Fire Department

ISBN/EAN: 9783337255398

Printed in Europe, USA, Canada, Australia, Japan

Cover: Foto ©Andreas Hilbeck / pixelio.de

More available books at **www.hansebooks.com**

REPORT

OF THE

Board of Fire Commissioners

Chief Engineer,

AND

Fire Alarm Superintendent

OF THE

San Francisco Fire Department

FOR THE

FISCAL YEAR ENDING JUNE 30, 1899

SAN FRANCISCO

THE HINTON PRINTING CO., 516 COMMERCIAL ST.

1899

REPORT

OF THE

BOARD OF FIRE COMMISSIONERS.

HEADQUARTERS FIRE DEPARTMENT,
OFFICE BOARD OF FIRE COMMISSIONERS
CITY HALL.

San Francisco, July 1, 1899

Gentlemen: In compliance with Resolution No. 2079 (Fourth Series) of your Honorable Body, the Board of Fire Commissioners herewith present and submit their Annual Report, containing a statement of the expenditures of the Department for the fiscal year ending June 30, 1899, also, Report of the Chief Engineer, showing the condition of the Department, a statement of the fires and alarms and their causes, and other information pertaining to the Department.

ORGANIZATION.

The Fire Department as now constituted consists of a Board of Fire Commissioners who act without compensation, a Chief Engineer, one First Assistant Chief Engineer, four Assistant Engineers, four Engineers of Relief Engines (acting as Assistant Engineers), thirty-four steam fire engine companies, seven hook and ladder companies, seven chemical engine companies, one water tower company, two monitor battery companies, and employees of office and Corporation Yard, composing a force of 568 men of all grades and positions.

RELIEF ENGINE COMPANIES.

In addition to said Companies, the Board of Fire Commissioners, on the 30th day of January, 1896, organized four steam fire engine companies for relief and emergency purposes, in pursuance of Order No. 2951 of the Board of Supervisors, and appointed four engineers for said companies at a salary of $140 per month each, and said engineers were thereafter detailed to perform the duties of Assistant Engineers, as above stated, in addition to the duties imposed on them by virtue of their positions in said relief engine companies. The remainder of the crews of said companies are detailed from the members and employees in service and employed in the Department, and serve without extra compensation.

6

FIRE COMMISSIONERS' REPORT.

UNIFORMED FORCE AND PAY-ROLL.

One Chief Engineer, salary per annum.....................................	$3,000
One Assistant Chief Engineer salary per annum............	2,400
4 Assistant Engineers, salary per annum, each............................	1,800
4 Engineers of Relief Engines (acting as Assistant Engineers), each.......................	1,680
34 Engineers of Steamers, each.	1,680
34 Stokers " "	1,080
34 Drivers " "	1,080
7 Drivers of Hook and Ladder Companies, each...........	1,080
7 Tillermen " " " "	1,080
7 Engineers of Chemical Engines, each................................	1,500
7 Drivers " " "	1,080
7 Firemen " " "	1,080
7 Stewards " " "	960
1 Engineer of Water Tower Co. No. 1................................	1,500
1 Driver of " "	1,080
1 Fireman of " "	1,080
2 Drivers of Monitor Batteries, each.................................	1,080

MEMBERS AT CALL, NOT UNIFORMED.

41 Foremen of Companies, each.................................	$540
272 Hosemen, each...	420
84 Hook and Ladder Men, each..........................	420

CORPORATION YARD EMPLOYEES.

1 Superintendent of Engines	$1,800
1 Assistant Superintendent of Engines	1,680
1 Engineer and Machinist..........................	1,680
1 Clerk of Corporation Yard..	1,500
1 Veterinary Surgeon..	720
2 Hydrantmen, each..................................	1,080
1 Carpenter..	1,200
1 Drayman..	1,080
1 Watchman..	900

Besides the regularly appointed employees of the Corporation Yard above mentioned there is an additional force of mechanics and laborers continually employed at the Yard and other workshops of the Department.

In conclusion, we herewith submit the annual report of the Chief Engineer, together with the reports from the various branches of this Department, to which your attention is specially invited.

Very respectfully submitted,
THE BOARD OF FIRE COMMISSIONERS,
GEO. MAXWELL, Secretary.

Report of the Chief Engineer

OF THE

San Francisco Fire Department.

Headquarters Fire Department,
City Hall,
San Francisco, Cal., July 1, 1899.

To the Honorable the Board of Fire Commissioners
  Of the City and County of San Francisco—

Gentlemen: I have the honor to present to you my annual report of the Fire Department of this City and County, together with such recommendations as in my judgment I deem necessary and proper to promote its efficiency.

REPORTS OF THE VARIOUS BRANCHES OF THE DEPARTMENT.

I herewith respectfully submit for your consideration the reports of the various branches of this Department, wherein you will find a correct statement and account of their respective operations during the fiscal year last past.

FIRES.

During the year the Department was called upon to respond to 508 alarms received from street and automatic boxes, of which 492 were first alarms, 11 second alarms, 4 third alarms and 1 fourth alarm; also, 320 silent alarms received verbally and by telephone, making a total of 828 alarms.

1

LOSSES BY FIRE, INSURANCE, AND AMOUNT PAID.

MONTH.	INSURANCE.	LOSS.	PAID.
1898.			
July	$445,723 00	$49,457 10	$41,028 85
August	128,143 00	25,022 94	19,793 69
September....................	121,100 00	15,663 00	14,023 00
October ....:.............................	146,650 00	26,656 21	25,366 21
November........	955,544 00	802,925 04	144,744 04
December...........................	114,550 00	5,308 45	4,768 45
1899.			
January...................................	399,400 00	51,244 85	41,163 01
February	310,107 00	32,309 21	29,991 21
March.........................	1,011,753 25	329,487 52	323,637 95
April	136,765 00	12,934 10	10,379 10
May..	206,675 00	26,694 06	23,834 06
June..	208,054 13	41,516 75	34,984 25
Total..	$4,184,464 38	$1,419,219 23	$713,713 82

STATEMENT OF NUMBER OF FEET OF MAIN PIPE LAID IN CITY FROM JULY 1
1898, TO JULY 1, 1899.

SIZE OF MAINS.	NUMBER OF FEET.	TAKEN OUT.	ABANDONED.
3-inch	458	120	
4-inch	6,112	5,086	817
6-inch	1,914	5,070	124
8-inch	57,256	922	68
10-inch		63	
12-inch	20,843	230	
16-inch	4,115	20	
20-inch	1,160		
22-inch			12
24-inch	975		
Total feet	92,833	11,511	1,721

Hydrants set..319
Hydrants re-set... 70
Hydrants taken out...148

Hydrants in use July 1, 1899.. 3,721

STATEMENT OF THE KIND OF APPARATUS, CLASS, NUMBER OF MEN AND

WORK DONE BY

COMPANY AND APPARATUS.	Class of Apparatus	No. of Men......	No. of Horses......
Engine Company No. 1, American, double............................	1	12	5
Engine Company No. 2, Metropolitan, double......................	2	12	5
Engine Company No. 3, Clapp & Jones, double....................	2	12	5
Engine Company No. 4, Metropolitan, double.....................	1	12	5
Engine Company No. 5, Clapp & Jones, double.....................	1	12	5
Engine Company No. 6, Clapp & Jones, double.	1	12	4
Engine Company No. 7, La France, double	3	12	5
Engine Company No. 8, La France, double...........................	2	12	5
Engine Company No. 9, Clapp & Jones, double	2	12	4
Engine Company No. 10, La France, double	1	12	5
Engine Company No. 11, Amoskeag, double.........................	2	12	5
Engine Company No. 12, La France, double.........................	1	12	5
Engine Company No. 13, La France, double	3	12	5
Engine Company No. 14, Metropolitan, double......................	3	12	5
Engine Company No. 15, La France, double	3	12	5
Engine Company No. 16, Amoskeag, double..................... ...	2	12	5
Engine Company No. 17. American, double......	1	12	5
Engine Company No. 18, La France, double........................	4	12	5
Engine Company No 19, Metropolitan, double...............	2	12	5
Engine Company No 20, Clapp & Jones, double.....................	3	12	5
Engine Company No. 21, Amoskeag, double.........................	2	12	5
Engine Company No. 22, La France, double	3	12	5
Engine Company No. 23, La France, double	4	12	5
Engine Company No. 24, La France, double.........................	4	12	5
Engine Company No. 25, Amoskeag, double	2	12	5
Engine Company No. 26, La France, double	4	12	5
Engine Company No. 27, Amoskeag, double	2	12	5
Engine Company No. 28, Clapp & Jones, double.....................	2	12	5
Engine Company No. 29, Amoskeag, double........................	1	12	5
Engine Company No. 30, La France, double.........................	4	12	5

HORSES, KIND OF HOSE, SIZE AND NUMBER OF FEET IN EACH COMPANY,

COMPANIES, ETC.

HOSE.			No. of Alarms Responded to...	No. of Fires Performed Duty at...	No. Still Alarms...	TIME WORKED.	
Kind.....	No. feet....	Size....				Hours....	Minutes....
Cotton.......	1,400	2¾-inch.	80	13	5	40	15
Cotton.......	1,400	2¾-inch.	140	33	5	48	20
Cotton.......	1,400	2¾-inch.	67	17	10	42	15
Cotton.......	1,350	3 -inch.	134	30	....	89	....
Cotton.......	1,400	2¾-inch.	100	48	29	42	20
Cotton.	1,300	3 -inch.	123	27	1	83	....
Cotton.......	1,400	2¾-inch.	46	16	4	39	50
Cotton.......	1,400	2¾-inch.	36	14	11	31	15
Cotton.......	1,400	2¾-inch.	53	23	9	76	5
Cotton.......	1,400	3 -inch.	92	32	5	86	15
Cotton.......	1,775	2½-inch.	16	7	2	26	30
Cotton.......	1,200	3 -inch.	82	18	5	44	25
Cotton.......	1,600	2¾-inch.	56	15	5	27	5
Cotton.......	1,600	2¾-inch.	53	8	19	26	30
Cotton.......	1,400	2½-inch.	47	11	8	12	15
Cotton.......	1,600	2½-inch.	23	14	6	54	....
Cotton....,.	1,400	3 -inch.	165	23	12	59	45
Cotton.......	1,850	2¾-inch.	23	12	2	17	15
Cotton.......	1,430	2¾-inch.	96	14	3	41	15
Cotton.......	1,600	2½-inch.	16	9	6	17	20
Cotton.......	1,650	2½-inch.	21	9	6	19	....
Cotton.......	1,650	2½-inch.	55	10	8	21	45
Cotton.......	1,630	2½-inch.	30	9	5	22	25
Cotton.......	1,600	2½-inch.	15	5	2	9	15
Cotton.......	1,600	2¾-inch.	54	15	6	32	15
Cotton.......	1,600	2½-inch.	22	11	8	12	....
Cotton.......	1,650	2½-inch.	37	14	4	25	15
Cotton.......	1,400	2¾-inch.	36	11	7	30	10
Cotton.......	1,450	3- inch.	62	17	6	53	30
Cotton.......	1,600	2½-inch.	12		5	10	30

STATEMENT OF THE KIND OF APPARATUS, CLASS, NUMBER OF MEN AND WORK DONE BY

Company and Apparatus.	Class of Apparatus.	Number of Men....	No. of Horses....
Engine Company No. 31, Metropolitan, double	3	12	5
Engine Company No. 32, La France, double	4	12	5
Engine Company No. 33, Amoskeag, single	3	12	5
Engine Company No. 34, La France, double	3	12	5
Truck Company No. 1, Straight Frame	1	15	3
Truck Company No. 2, Straight Frame	1	15	3
Truck Company No. 3, Straight Frame	3	15	3
Truck Company No. 4, Straight Frame	3	15	3
Truck Company No. 5, Straight Frame	3	15	3
Truck Company No. 6, Straight Frame	3	15	3
Truck Company No. 7, Straight Frame	3	15	3
Chemical Engine No. 1, Champion, double sixty	....	4	2
Chemical Engine No. 2, Hose Wagon	....	4	2
Chemical Eugine No. 3, Champion, double eighty	....	4	2
Chemical Engine No. 4, Champion, double sixty	....	4	2
Chemical Engine No 5, Champion, double sixty	....	4	2
Chemical Engine No 6, Champion, double sixty	....	4	2
Chemical Engine No 7, Champion, double one hundred	....	4	2
Water Tower Company No. 1, Gorter Tower	1	3	3
Monitor Battery No. 1	....	1	1
Monitor Battery No. 2	....	1	1

HORSES, KIND OF HOSE, SIZE AND NUMBER OF FEET IN EACH COMPANY, COMPANIES, ETC.—CONCLUDED.

Hose.			No. of Alarms Responded to....	No. of Fires Performed Duty at..	No. Still Alarms...	Time Worked.	
Kind......	No. feet....	Size......				Hours....	Minutes....
Cotton.......	1,400	2¾-inch.	53	10	1	24	20
Cotton.......	1,400	2½-inch.	42	15	5	20	5
Cotton.......	2,000	2½-inch.	10	10	8	16	20
Cotton......	1,400	2¾-inch.	70	5	1	11	35
Cotton......	200	1 -inch.	137	70	6	108	15
Cotton.......	200	1 -inch.	85	65	18	93	15
Cotton......	200	1 -inch.	118	78	7	128	15
Cotton.......	100	1 -inch.	38	30	11	44	45
Cotton.......	100	1 -inch.	54	35	9	34	45
Cotton.......	100	1 -inch.	22	16	11	72	50
Cotton......	100	1 -inch.	87	48	6	87	15
Rubber......	250	1 -inch.	123	82	28	60	30
Cotton.......	1,600	2½-inch.	2	2	2	5	30
Rubber......	250	1 -inch.	38	25	12	23	....
Rubber......	250	1 -inch.	87	50	20	46	25
Rubber......	250	1 -inch.	57	51	25	50	20
Rubber......	250	1 -inch.	84	56	24	39	20
Rubber......	200	1 -inch.	58	44	8	33	45
....	....	....	82	6	....	16	....
....	....	....	68	2	....	7	35
....	....	....	66	1	....	5	45

NEW HOUSES.

During the year the following new houses were built:

Engine House No. 35—Two-story frame building, with basement; situate at Holly Park and West avenues.

Chemical Engine House No. 2—Two-story frame building, with basement; situate at No. 1348 Tenth avenue.

The erection of Engine House No. 36—a three-story brick building, with basement—situate on the north side of Bluxome street, between Fourth and Fifth streets, was also commenced.

NEW DRILL TOWER.

A new drill tower, with all the necessary equipments, was erected in the rear of Engine House No. 28, at the southwest corner of Francisco and Stockton streets.

REAL ESTATE.

The Department purchased the following described pieces of property during the year, to wit:

Commencing at a point on the northwesterly line of Bluxome street, 230 feet southwest from the northwest corner of Fourth and Bluxome sts.; running thence southwesterly along said line of Bluxome street 50 feet; thence at right angles northwesterly 120 feet; thence at right angles northeasterly 50 feet, and thence at right angles southeasterly 120 feet to the point of commencement.

Commencing at a point on the northwesterly line of Howard street, distant thereon 160 feet northeast of the northeast line of Third street, and running thence northeasterly along said northwest line of Howard street 40 feet; thence at right angles northwest 110 feet to the southeast line of Hunt street; thence southwest along the southeast line of Hunt street 40 feet, and thence at right angles southeast 110 feet to the point of beginning.

NEW APPARATUS.

The following new apparatus was purchased, to wit: 4 steam fire engines, 10 hose wagons, 2 monitor batteries, 1 combination chemical engine and hose wagon, and 1 combination chemical engine and hook and ladder truck.

NEW HOSE.

The Department purchased new hose as follows: 5,600 feet of 2 3-4 inch Victor Jacket, 400 feet of 3 inch Victor Jacket, 200 feet of 3 1-2 inch Victor Jacket, 500 feet of 1 1-2 inch Victor Jacket, 500 feet of 1 inch 4-ply Chemical.

NEW WATER TOWER.

A new water tower is now in course of construction at the workshop of the Department, under the supervision of H. H. Gorter, master machinist.

APPARATUS.

The apparatus of the Department, all in good condition, consists of 50 steam fire engines, 11 hook and ladder trucks, 9 chemical engines, 2 water towers, 4 monitor batteries, 53 hose wagons, 1 combination chemical engine and hose wagon, 50 Babcock hand chemical extinguishers, and 65,800 feet of cotton hose.

CONDITION OF ENGINE HOUSES.

All the engine houses are in good condition except Engine Houses Nos. 9, 22, 23 and 24.

HORSES.

There are at present in service in the Department 292 horses, including those kept for relief, and three colts.

With the exception of 18 that are now under treatment at the hospital for various ailments, and 5 that are being treated at the engine houses for minor troubles that do not necessitate their being put out of service, they are all in good condition.

During the year 39 horses were purchased, 29 condemned as being unfit for service, 23 of which were sold at public auction, the remaining 6 being transferred to Branch County Jail No. 2 by order of the Board of Supervisors.

Six horses were shot on account of broken legs, 1 for injured spine, and 6 died from sickness at the hospital, making a total of 13 deaths during the year.

HARNESS, BLANKETS AND BITS.

The harness, blankets and bits throughout the Department are all in first-class condition.

TRANSFER OF COMPANIES.

Engine Company No. 32—From 3050 Seventeenth street to new engine house at Holly Park and West avenues.

Truck Company No. 7—From Engine House No. 25, 2547 Folsom street, and Chemical Engine Company No. 7, from Engine House No. 7, 3160 Sixteenth street, to Engine House No. 32.

TRANSFER OF APPARATUS, ETC.

By authority of the Board of Supervisors, the apparatus, hose, etc., hereinafter specified was transferred as follows:

To the Sutro Estate (for fire protection at Sutro Heights and vicinity)—One relief Amoskeag steam fire engine, with suctions and engine tools.

To the Alms House—One steam fire engine, one hose cart, and 1,800 feet of hose.

To the Street Department—250 feet of hose.

To the Fire Alarm and Police Telegraph—400 feet of hose, 2 horses, 1 set of harness and 1 wagon.

SALE OF OLD HORSES AND MATERIAL.

During the year, upon the recommendation of the Board of Fire Commissioners, and by authortiy of the Board of Supervisors, the Mayor sold, as provided by law, 17 old horses, 1 old gas engine and a lot of old material, consisting of old engine boilers, cast and wrought iron scraps, etc., and the proceeds of such sales, amounting to $704.30, was paid into the City Treasury to the credit of the Fire Department Fund.

FIRE PROTECTION FOR SUTRO HEIGHTS AND VICINITY.

By Resolution No. 3031 (Fourth Series) of the Board of Supervisors, approved June 29, 1899, the petition of the executors of the Sutro Estate, offering the use of a suitable house near Sutro Heights for an engine company, and all extra help needed, together with the necessary horses, harness and feed, upon condition that the City loan a steam fire engine, with necessary equipments, and employ an engineer and driver therefor, was, upon recommendation of the Board of Fire Commissioners, approved and accepted, and, in accordance therewith, an engine company was organized and placed in service thereat.

ROLL OF HONOR.

On January 19, 1899, a Roll of Honor was, upon my recommendation, established in this Department, for the inscription of the names of the recipients of the "Scannell" or other special medal for bravery, and of others who may perform acts of valor deserving public recognition, whose names may be ordered inscribed thereon by the Board of Fire Commissioners.

"THE MERCHANTS' ASSOCIATION MEDAL FOR HEROISM."

On the 1st of December, 1898, the Merchants' Association of this City, by the following communication addressed to the Board of Fire Commissioners, kindly agreed to donate two gold medals to this Department, to be awarded as therein provided:

San Francisco, December 1, 1898.

To the Honorable the Board of Fire Commissioners
Of the City and County of San Francisco—

Gentlemen: The Merchants' Association desires publicly to express its high appreciation of the invaluable services rendered by the San Francisco Fire Department upon the many memorable occasions in the annals of our City. The heroic conduct displayed at the recent Baldwin Hotel fire by the officers and men of the Department in rescuing hundreds of imperiled lives at their own imminent peril has immortalized their names, while the masterly manner in which this conflagration was confined and conquered challenges universal admiration.

As a fitting though inadequate recognition of the superb efficiency and indomitable courage of the officers and men of the San Francisco Fire Department, the Merchants' Association hereby agrees to provide two gold medals, to be awarded on January 1, 1899, and on January 1, 1900, respectively (or on such other dates as your Honorable Board may decide), to the two members of the Fire Department deemed most worthy by reason of exceptionally heroic conduct during the respective years.

We beg to tender this token without any conditions, except that "The Merchants' Association Medal for Heroism" be awarded by vote of a majority of your Honorable Board, and that its presentation to the distinguished recipients be made publicly, in the presence of as many as possible of the members of the Department.

Trusting that this medal may serve in some degree to stimulate devotion to duty and commemorate immortal deeds, we remain,

Faithfully yours,

(Signed)   MERCHANTS' ASSOCIATION.
J. RICH'D FREUD, Secretary.   F. W. DOHRMANN, President.

AWARD OF THE "SCANNELL MEDALS" AND "THE MERCHANTS' ASSOCIATION MEDAL FOR HEROISM."

On the 22d day of February, 1899, Frederick Sayers of Engine 1, James Cumisky of Truck 6, and Assistant Engineer P. H. Shaughnessy were awarded medals of honor in recognition of heroism displayed in saving life at the Baldwin Hotel fire on the morning of the 23d day of November, 1898.

Sayers rescued A. H. Christie, of Milwaukee, from the cornice of the fifth floor of the burning hotel, coming upon him just as he was about to end his suffering in despair by cutting his throat with a razor, and carrying him down a fire escape ladder to a place of safety.

Cumisky and Shaughnessy rescued an unknown woman from the flames, which had seemingly cut off all hope of her escape from the fifth floor.

The presentation of the medals was made publicly, at Metropolitan Temple, upon which occasion a large number of comrades of the recipients were also present. There were but two Scannell Medals available, but the Merchants' Association of this City kindly donated and provided two gold medals, one of which was awarded upon this occasion in order that all three of the firemen who had won extraordinary distinction might be suitably and similarly rewarded. Mayor Phelan, in an eloquent address, presented the Scannell Medals to Sayers and Cumisky, and Mr. F. W. Dohrmann, President of the Merchants' Association, likewise presented the Merchants' Association Medal for Heroism to Assistant Engineer Shaughnessy.

PROMOTIONS.

Upon my recommendation, the following promotions were made during the year, viz:

Patrick Barry, from Foreman of Engine 15 to Fireman of Engine 23.

Fred Whitaker, from Assistant Foreman to Foreman of Engine 15.

Charles Nell, from Watchman Corporation Yard to Fireman of Engine 10.

Joseph Sawyer, from Truckman of Truck 3 to Watchman Corporation Yard.

Michael Boden, from Assistant Foreman to Foreman of Engine 2.

Frederick Sayers, from Assistant Foreman to Foreman of Engine 1.

Frank Sullivan, from Hoseman of Engine 29 to Steward Chemical 6.

Chris Ward, from Hoseman of Engine 3 to Fireman of Engine 26.

Maurice Barrett, from Hoseman of Engine 25 to Steward Chemical 1.

Maurice Barrett, from Steward of Chemical 1 to Driver of Engine 20.

C. J. Hogan, from Hoseman of Engine 13 to Foreman of Engine 16.

James Minnigan, from Hoseman of Engine 10 to Steward of Chemical 3.

Nicholas Barbetta, from Steward of Chemical 3 to Fireman of Engine 11.

Joseph Wales, from Hoseman of Engine 29 to Driver Monitor Battery 2.

RETIRED ON PENSION.

Four members were retired under the provisions of the Firemen's Pension Fund Act, viz.:

James Mason, Engineer of Engine Co. No. 33, retired August 11, 1898, because of age, infirmity, and disability of a permanent character which incapacitated him from performing any further duty in the Department. He was in the service for 16 years.

John J. McGorry, Driver of Chemical Engine Co. No. 6, retired October 20, 1898, on account of sickness and disability contracted while in the service, which permanently incapacitated him from performing any further duty. He was a member of the Department for 17 years.

William Mulcahy, Hoseman of Engine Co. No. 19, retired December 15, 1898, because of permanent disability, caused by injuries received in the discharge of his duties. He was in the service for 19 years.

Patrick McCormick, Foreman of Engine Co. No. 16, retired February 16, 1899, because of age, infirmity, and disability caused by exposure while engaged in the service. He was a member of the Department for 21 years.

DEATHS.

Hugh Monaghan, Hoseman of Engine 1, died September 15, 1898, of pneumonia.

John Kavanagh, Truckman of Truck 5, met his death by drowning in the bay on September 21, 1898.

Michael Kelleher, Substitute member of Truck 3, was killed October 30, 1898, by falling from a ladder while at a drill.

Joseph P. Gross, Hoseman of Engine 5, died November 30, 1898, from the result of a gun-shot wound.

John Burnell, Hoseman of Engine 2, died January 21, 1899, of pneumonia.

John J. McGorry (retired on pension), died April 20, 1899, of liver complaint.

John Cook (retired on pension), died May 15, 1899, of paralysis.

Benjamin Whitehead (retired on pension), died May 31, 1899, of a complication of diseases.

NOTABLE FIRES.

July 29, 1898. Box 19. This fire occurred at about 11.25 p. m., in a cheap lodging house, a three-story frame structure, at 113 Oregon st., and resulted in the death by smothering and burning of five people, and the serious injury of five others. That there were no more fatalities is remarkable, as there were over twenty people asleep in the house at the time, and the fire, which was not discovered until it had gained considerable headway, spread through the building with great rapidity, doing damage in every room in all three stories. A number of the inmates escaped death or serious injury by jumping from the windows, and but one of these was injured by leaping to the ground.

The fire was confined to this building and subdued in a short time. Cause, explosion of a coal oil lamp. Loss to building and contents, $800. No insurance.

November 21, 1898. Box 294. At 7.45 o'clock on this evening the Department responded to a call for a fire in a Chinese lodging house, at 20-24 Waverly place. Two policemen, who discovered the fire, gave warning to the inmates, a large number of whom hurried into the street. The Department worked in the building for some time, and had the fire well under control, when the bodies of two Chinamen were discovered in their bunks burned to death. Cause, overturning or explosion of coal oil lamp. Loss, $3,500, covered by insurance.

November 23, 1898. At about 3.20 o'clock on the morning of this day, an alarm was given from Box 47 for a fire in the Baldwin Hotel, a six-story building of brick and wood, situate at the junction of Market, Powell and Eddy streets. The fire spread with remarkable rapidity, and immediately upon the arrival cf the Department a third alarm was sent in, followed by a fourth a few moments later. By this time the entire upper floor was a mass of flames, and the theatre in the building a roaring furnace. The hotel was filled with guests, and a number of firemen, assisted by the police, made their way into the blind corridors and smoking hallways to arouse the sleeping people. Great excitement followed as the flames leaped and roared, and men and women made their appearance at windows and on cornices of the building, piteously calling for assistance. Thousands of people crowded the streets in every direction, cheering the firemen as they proceeded in their work of rescuing the guests, whose lives were in danger. It became apparent that there was no hope of saving the hotel, and the efforts of the Department were directed towards saving the surrounding property, which, after a hard struggle, was accomplished, and the fire was confined to the building where it originated. Several guests unfortunately met their death at this fire, and three victims thereof were treated at the City Receiving Hospital for injuries received.

The Baldwin Hotel has been known and dreaded for years as a fire trap, and a menace to the lives of those who lived in it.

The fire is supposed to have started in the hotel kitchen, which was located on the second floor of the Ellis street side.

The building was totally destroyed. Loss, $791,344.

January 1, 1899. Box 261. Second Alarm. The machinery and plant of the Krough Manufacturing Company, makers of pumps and hydraulic machinery, and the factory of the California Artistic Metal & Wire Works were totally destroyed by this fire. The two concerns occupied one building at 9-17 Stevenson street.

Cause, spontaneous combustion. Loss, $21,000, partly covered by insurance.

January 29, 1899. Box 281. This fire destroyed the San Bruno Hotel, a laborers' boarding house, on the San Bruno road, near Army street. Mathias Eichorn, an aged Swiss, was burned to death, and a number of firemen were slightly injured.

February 12, 1899. Box 21. Fireworks exploded in celebration of the Chinese New Year by the Alaska Packing Co., at 724 Commercial street, set fire to the building, completely destroying the contents of the second story; burned one Chinaman to death, and badly scorched three others.

March 31, 1899. Box 261. Third Alarm. This fire occurred in the hardware establishment of Miller, Sloss & Scott, a five-story brick building at 18-22 Fremont street. Cause, carelessness in smoking. Loss, $299,216.90, covered by insurance.

RECOMMENDATIONS.

I renew my recommendation that the Department be reorganized into a fully paid system, with the entire force continually on duty.

The force should be increased to at least thirty-five steam fire engine companies, nine truck companies, seven chemical engine companies, two water tower companies, one fire-boat company, and two monitor battery companies.

Engine houses Nos. 9, 22 and 24 should be torn down, and new, modern structures erected in their places, and Engine house No. 23 should be repaired.

In view of the immense value of shipping interests of this City, better protection should be given to the water front, and I therefore earnestly recommend that a light-draught, high-power fire-boat of good speed and large pumping capacity be provided for that purpose. Hundreds of thousands of dollars might be saved to the community by the expenditure of comparatively few thousands in this direction.

All engine houses should be lighted by electricity, and the latest appliances employed for that purpose.

The silent system of signals and new switchboards should be provided in all fire houses of the Department.

The latest improved keyless doors should be placed on the fire-boxes in the mercantile district, as a means of saving much valuable time in turning in alarms of fire.

I again recommend the immediate removal of the Fire Alarm Office to some suitable place in the City Hall, and the purchase of a proper plant for the conduct of this important branch of the Fire Department. In its present location the office is in great danger of being destroyed by fire, together with its valuable appliances, and should be located in a more safe position.

I also recommend that the water supply throughout the City be increased by the removal of all small and inadequate water mains, and replacing them with eight, twelve, sixteen and twenty-four inch mains in all portions of the City not already supplied with mains of large and sufficient capacity; and more fire hydrants should be set in all districts that are not sufficiently provided therewith. I further recommend that all cisterns now available for fire purposes be repaired, and that one hundred additional underground reservoirs, with capacities of not less than 10,000 gallons, be built on the corners of streets in the hotel and mercantile districts, and fed by eight-inch pipes with gate valves attached directly from the street mains. By this means many more engines could be stationed nearer fires, and their streams, siamesed into one large stream, would enable the Department to fight fires more effectively.

In closing this report, I desire to tender my thanks to your Honorable Board for the active interest manifested by you in all matters pertaining to the success of the Department, and I also desire to thank the officers and members of the force for the alacrity manifested by them on all occasions in complying with my orders. I also desire to express my thanks to His Honor Mayor Phelan and the Honorable Board of Supervisors for the interest they have manifested in all business pertaining to the Department. To the Chief of Police and members of his force, to Fire Marshal Charles Towe, to Captain Comstock of the Underwriters' Fire Patrol, and to Superintendent Hewitt of the Fire Alarm Office, I am under many obligations for the manner in which they have assisted this Department in the discharge of their duties on all occasions. Very respectfully yours,

D. T. SULLIVAN,
Chief Engineer of the Fire Department.

REPORT OF THE VARIOUS BRANCHES OF THE DEPARTMENT.

REPORT OF SUPERINTENDENT OF ENGINES.

San Francisco, July 1, 1899.

To the Honorable the Board of Fire Commissioners and the Chief Engineer—

Gentlemen: I respectfully report the following repairs, alterations and additions to the Department at Corporation Yards Nos. 1 and 2, during the Fiscal Year ending June 30, 1899:

1 Engine bed lathe, 24-inch swing; 1 engine bed lathe, 14-inch swing; 1 engine bed lathe, 16-inch swing, with Monitor attachment; 1 drill press; 1 emery grinder; 1 15-inch shaper; 1 milting tool, No. 3; 2 electric motors; 1 combination hose wagon and chemical engine; 1 combination truck wagon and chemical engine; 10 hose wagons; 1 supply wagon; 1 small wagon (Delivery); 4 steam fire engines; 2 Monitor batterys, built at Corporation Yard; 4 three-horse hitches; 2 buggies; 4 forward gears for engines with platform springs; 20 electric let goes; 4 wheels (Archibald patterns) for chemical engines rebuilt; 1 Hayes truck; 1 La France engine; 1 Clapp and Jones engine; 1 wagon; 2 delivery wagons; 3 hydrant carts; 2 stable wagons; 1 Carpt. shop wagon; feed cooking plant at Department Stable placed in service; 19 3-inch Siamese connections, with bladed play pipes; 10 3-inch three way connections, with bladed play pipes. A standee adjusted to each pipe.

The following pieces of apparatus have been repaired during the year, some of them many times:

Engines Nos. 1, 2, 3, 4, 5, 6, 7, 8, 9, 10, 11, 12, 13, 14, 15, 16, 17, 18, 19, 20, 21, 22, 23, 24, 25, 26, 27, 28, 29, 30, 31, 32, 33, 34.

Relief Engines Nos 1, 2, 3, 4, 5, 6, 7, 8, 9, 10, 11, 12, 13.

Hose Wagons Nos. 1, 2, 3, 4, 5, 6, 7, 8, 9, 10, 11, 12, 13, 14, 15, 16, 17, 18, 19, 20, 21, 22, 23, 24, 25, 26, 27, 28, 29, 30, 31, 32, 33, 34.

Relief Hose wagons Nos. 1, 2, 3, 4, 5, 6, 7, 8, 9, 10, 11, 12, 13, 14, 15, 16, 17.

Chemical Engines Nos. 1, 2, 3, 4, 5, 6, 7.

Relief Chemical Engines Nos. 1, 2, 3.

Water Towers Nos. 1, 2.

Trucks Nos. 1, 2, 3, 4, 5, 6, 7.

Relief Trucks Nos. 1, 2, 3, 4.

Corporation Yard Wagons Nos. 1, 2, 3.

Hydrant Man Carts Nos. 1, 2, 3, 4.

Stable Wagons—4.

District Engineers' Buggies—15.

Carpenter Shop Wagons—2.

Also blacksmithing machine and heater work, together with plumbing, tinning, etc., for the various houses throughout the Department.

The following will show the capacity of all Engines in use by this Department:

APPARATUS.	PUMP	STROKE.	CAPACITY PER MINUTE.
4 Engines	5¼-inch.	9-inch.	944 gallons.
5 Engines	5½-inch.	8-inch.	940 gallons.
1 Engines	4⅓-inch.	8-inch.	700 gallons.
1 Engine	4½-inch.	12-inch.	740 gallons.
1 Engine	4½-inch.	8-inch.	640 gallons.
15 Engines	4¼-inch.	8-inch.	585 gallons.
2 Engines	4⅞-inch.	6-inch.	540 gallons.
2 Engines	4⅝-inch.	8-inch.	300 gallons.
1 Engine.	4⅜-inch.	12-inch.	400 gallons.
4 Engines	4½-inch.	7-inch.	575 gallons.
3 Engines	5-inch.	7-inch.	708 gallons.
6 Engines	4-inch.	7-inch.	460 gallons.
2 Engines	5-inch.	8-inch.	400 gallons.
1 Engine.	5½-inch.	9-inch.	520 gallons.

I would earnestly recommend the early retirement of all single engines from the service, they being much more severe on hose and suction than the type of double engines now being built.

Respectfully submitted,

J. W. REILLY,

Superintendent of Engines.

REPORT OF DEPARTMENT CARPENTER.

San Francisco, July 1, 1899.

To the Honorable the Board of Fire Commissioners and the Chief Engineer—

Gentlemen: The following is a list of carpenter work performed in this department during the Fiscal Year ending June 30, both by contract and by the department carpenter:

BY CONTRACT.

No. 35 Engine house, No. 2 Chemical house, and No. 2 Drill Tower, steel frame.

BY DEPARTMENT CARPENTER (COSTING FROM $200 AND UP.)

Engine houses Nos. 1, 2, 3, 20, 24, 25, 11, 35, 28 Annex, No. 4 Chemical, No. 2 Corporation Yard, Drill Tower, stables and carpenter shop.

No. 1 Engine—Built new brick wall around lot in the rear of building; planked yard; built large shed; tore out the rear end of main building; enlarged door way; made new doors and hung same, etc.

No. 2 Engine—Tore out old floor, stalls, etc.; put in new floor, new stalls, with guards on floor instead of posts and partitions; repaired all doors, windows, etc.

No. 3 Engine—Tore out front of Battery house in the rear of main building, and enlarged same 10 feet; built a new front and remodeled the whole building; replanked yard; repaired bulkhead, stalls, doors, windows, etc.

No. 11 Engine—Tore down part of old building, and built new house, 25 x 70 ft., two stories; 1st story, walls and ceiling sheathed with 1 x 4 T. & G. Bd. Rw.; 2d story, walls and ceiling plastered; built 9 stationary lockers, bathroom, 2 water closets, 2 slide poles, spiral stairs, 5 stalls, sink; enlarged heater room, and put in concrete floor; sheathed walls of same with 1-inch Rw.; new stairs to same. Cemented walls and floor of manure pit, and new iron doors. The old building left standing required a great many repairs, as follows: One entire new side, new shingle roof; many repairs on the front and bulkhead and plank yard. The Hose and Bell Tower we repaired with some new sills, new studding, rustic and braces.

No. 20 Engine—Tore out the whole of first story, except brick foundation, and put in new sills, studding, floor joists, floor stalls; enclosed with new rustic. First story sheathed with 1 x 4 T. & G. Bd. Rw.; put in new ventilators 3 feet square in front, rear and sides of building; repaired yard, door, windows, etc. Also fitted up qarters for Engine Company while this house was under repairs.

No. 24 Engine—Put in new floor and stalls; repaired front doors, and put on new hinges, etc.

No. 25 Engine—Tore out floor and floor joists, sills; cut out studding and sheathing, and replaced with new material; built new stalls; put in 5 ventilators, 20 inches by 36 inches, in floor and sides of building; repaired all doors and windows, etc.

No. 28 Engine Annex—Graded lot 31 ft. by 65 ft. 12 inches deep for the foundation; put up building full size of lot, one story high, with tin roof; sheathed inside with 1 x 4 T. & G. Bd. Rw.; 2 large sliding doors, front and rear; 3 windows; 5 stalls; planked yard, etc.

No. 35 Engine—Put in iron rods to strengthen hay loft; tore out the front of all stalls; took off doors, and made more room to allow the horses to get in and out of stalls; built runway in front of house 40 ft. long; enclosed shed in yard; put new springs on front doors, etc.

Stables—Layed new floor in front and rear part of stables; tore out wagon wash stand in the rear of building, and repaired the one in the front; built new shed, 10 x 55 ft. in front of stables for engine and wagon; rustic on outside; cornice on the front and side; tin roof; sliding door, etc.; also repaired all doors and windows in main building.

No. 4 Chemical House—Moved house from Eddy and Polk streets to McAllister, between Van Ness and Polk streets. Built new brick foundations for the building, and new heater room 20 x 24 ft. with concrete floor; enlarged building thirty feet, which now makes house 25 x 70 ft.; tore out rear end of building, and added to and remodeled the whole inside of house; sheathed first and second stories with 1 x 4 T. & G. Bd. Rw.; put in iron spiral stairs, new front doors, 5 stalls; second story partitioned into dormitory, sitting room, bath room, water closet; put in 6 new windows, 4 doors, 1 sliding pole; planked yard and alley way; built new fence and shed in yard 18 x 30 ft. with rustic on sides; cornice; tin roof and sliding doors.

No. 2 Drill Tower—Built 124 ft. tight board fence 7 ft. high around lot where Drill Tower is built; planked yard 34 x 130 ft. with 3-inch pine plank; cased around floor joists of each story of tower with 1-inch Rw.; built room for architect on second floor of Tower; built plumb wall 12 x 82 inches, with 10 windows to drill with Pomppii ladders; put double roof over second and fifth stories; spiral stairs to second story.

No. 2 Corporation Yard—Fitted up part of No. 2 Corporation Yard for machine shop. 1st floor—Built galleries 10 x 50 ft.; put up 150 feet shafting, and room for dynamo. 2d story—Built gallery 22 x 30 ft.; tightened all bolts in truss of roof; tore out and made doorway wider in rear of building; built shed in yard 20 x 34 ft.; rustic on outside; cornice, and tin roof.

Carpenter Shop—Besides sizing and surfacing lumber, making brackets, cornices, etc., for the different houses built and repaired this year by the Department Carpenter, there has been made in the shop, 21 extension ladders, 22 ft. long; 14 straight ladders, 9 ft. long; 14 loft ladders, 12 ft. long; 24 French ladders; 24 step ladders; 10 beding wagons; 12 shaving boxes; 12 acid cradles; 24 lockers; 12 record boards; 4 set double front doors; 3 heavy single doors; 100 weight boxes. Have run about 80,000 feet 2 x 4 T. & G. pine; 6,000 feet 1 x 6 T. & G. Bd. Rw.; 500 ladder rings; 125 hydrant plugs; 100 plugs for hose pipe; 2,000 ft. 1 x 6¼ round casings; 8,500 ft. assorted mouldings.

Respectfully submitted,

JOHN DOYLE,

Acting Carpenter San Francisco Fire Department.

REPORT OF DEPARTMENT PAINTER.

San Francisco, July 1, 1899.

To the Honorable the Board of Fire Commissioners and the Chief Engineer—

Gentlemen: Following is the report of the Paint Department of goods delivered and received, and apparatus, etc., painted by this department from July 1, 1898, to July 1, 1800:

APPARATUS, ETC., PAINTED.

Painted buggy for Chief Sullivan.
Painted dashboard for Hydrantman Quinlan.
Painted six iron beds for Engine No. 4.
Painted and lettered blackboard for Engine No. 12.
Painted Relief Chemical.
Painted new work on delivery wagon No. 2.
Touched up and varnished Engineer Sullivan's relief buggy.
Painted buggy for District Engineer McCloskey.
Touched up and varnished Hydrantman Rice's buggy.
Painted new work on Assistant Chief Dougherty's buggy.
Lettered and varnished apron for Engine No. 4.
Painted shafts for stable buggy.
Painted white hat for District Engineer Shaugnessy.
Painted new work on harnessmaker's wagon.
Painted apron for Chemical No. 4.
Painted Water Tower No. 2.
Painted buggy for District Engineer Dolan.
Painted white hat for District Engineer Dolan.
Painted Relief Hose Wagon No. 53.
Painted Ladder Hose Wagon No. 11.
Painted extension ladder and braces on Wagon No. 16.
Painted Truck No. 4.
Painted Relief Hose Wagon No. 42.
Painted cart for Hydrantman Riley.
Painted cart for Hydrantman Quinlan.
Painted new buggy for Assistant Chief Dougherty.
Touched up and varnished District Engineer Conlon's buggy.
Painted Bangor Ladder Relief.
Painted new work on Hose Wagon No. 31.
Painted new work on Hose Wagon No. 3.
Painted Relief Buggy.
Painted set of engine wheels.
Painted and lettered apron for Water Tower No. 2.
Painted new work on Engine No. 3.
Painted new work on Hose Wagon No. 36.
Painted Hose Wagon No. 27.
Painted sign for plumbing shop.
Painted new buggy for District Engineer Fernandez.
Painted new work on Hose Wagon No. 17.

Painted Engine No. 18.
Painted cart for Hydrantman O'Connell.
Painted desk for Engineer Shaugnessy.
Painted buggy for stable.
Painted desk for Clerk Fleming.
Painted Relief Cart.
Painted coal box for Engine No. 1.
Painted tanks on Chemical No. 1.
Painted new work on Hose Wagon No. 21.
Painted and lettered Record Board, Yard No. 1.
Painted and lettered two Record Boards.
Painted new addition to Clerk Fleming's desk.
Painted Hose Wagon No. 37.
Painted District Engineer McCloskey's buggy.
Painted and lettered blackboard for Truck No. 7.
Painted new work on Relief Chemical No. 8.
Painted new work on Relief Engine No. 250.
Painted new work on Hose Wagon No. 7.
Painted new work on Hose Wagon No. 34.
Painted new buggy for Chief Sullivan.
Painted new work on Hose Wagon No. 33.
Painted Relief Buggy.
Painted new work on Hose Wagon No. 15.
Painted buggy for District Engineer Shaugnessy.
Painted new work on Hose Wagon No. 8.
Painted new work on Hose Wagon No. 47.
Painted new work on Hydrantman Riley's cart.
Lettered and Varnished 3 new Record Boards.
Painted 30 book racks for Engine Houses.
Painted Relief buggy.
Painted apron for Chemical No. 4.
Touched up and varnished Engine No. 31.
Painted buggy for District Engineer Wills.
Painted new work on Truck No. 6.
Painted white hat for Assistant Chief Dougherty.
Painted Truck No. 1.
Painted new work on District Engineer Shaugnessy's buggy.
Painted hind and front gear on Truck No. 8.
Touched up and varnished Engine No. 2.
Painted four frames for fire alarm cards.
Painted stable wagon No. 1.
Painted Hydrantman Brady's cart.
Painted and lettered blackboard for Chemical No. 2.
Painted carpenter wagon No. 11.
Touched up and varnished Hose Wagon No. 2.
Touched up and varnished District Engineer Dolan's buggy.
Painted two coats of lead on Ambulance.
Painted Relief Buggy No. 17.
Painted two small extension ladders.
Painted District Engineer McKittricks Buggy No. 7.
Painted two signs for Corporation Yards 1 and 2.
Painted four fire alarm frames.
Touched up and varnished Hose Wagon No. 20.
Painted set of ladders for new truck.
Painted 14 small extension ladders.

Painted new work on Hose Wagon No. 45.
Painted new wood for blue prints.
Painted new work on Chief Sullivan's shafts.
Painted new work on District Engineer Shaugnessy's buggy.
Painted new work on Chemical No. 7.
Painted trumpet for Assistant Chief Dougherty.
Painted new work on Truck No. 4.
Painted new work on buggy No. 17.
Painted new work on Hose Wagon No. 44.
Painted Battery No. 1.
Painted new work on Engine No. 25.
Painted Relief Buggy.
Painted District Engineer Conlon's buggy No. 8.
Painted Hose Wagon No. 4.
Painted new work on Engine No. 5.
Painted new work on Relief Engine.
Painted Battery No. 3.
Touched up body and painted gear Hose Wagon Nc. 1.
Painted frame for fire alarm card.
Painted brake block Chemical No. 2.
Painted new work on Truck No. 1, new truck.
Painted new work on Engine No. 31.
Painted Hydrantman Rice's buggy.
Touched up body, painted gear Hose Wagon No. 34.
Painted new work on Hose Wagons 19, 16, 34, 15, 6.
Painted new work on Truck No. 1.
Painted and lettered blackboard Corporation Yard No. 2.
Touched up and varnished, relettered, 16 Record Boards.

GOODS RECEIVED FROM JULY 1, 1898, TO JULY 1, 1899.

DATE.	NAME.	ARTICLES.
898—July 1	Wm. P. Fuller & Co......	8 lbs. Coopers' Glue, 5 lbs. Blue Dry.
July 5	J. J. Mack & Co..............	1 Dozen Bottles Strong Ammonia.
July 8.............	Yates & Co..............	1 Gallon White Enamel, 1 2-in. Varnish Brush, 1 1-in. Varnish Brush, ½ Gallon Paint Remover, 1 Gallon Gasoline.
July 9.............	Dunham, Carrigan & Co	1 Screw Driver, 1 S. Wrench, 1 Alligator Wrench, 1 Bellows, 4 Granite Cups, 1 Dozen Tin Cups.
July 11.............	Wm. P. Fuller & Co......	2 Gallons Wearing Body Varnish, 2 Gallons Coach Rubbing Varnish, 1 4-oz. Bottle French Spirit Varnish, 1 Box Gold Paint.
July 11.............	Yates & Co..............	3 Tubes Vertigrease, 1 ½-in. Burnisher, 1 Wheel.
July 14.............	Yates & Co	12 Blocks Eureka Stone.
July 16.............	Wm. P. Fuller & Co	5 Gallons Boiled Oil.
July 16.............	Bass, Hueter & Co	10 oz. Bottle Gold Laque, 1 No. 16 Compass.
July 22.............	Yates & Co	1 Gallon Wood Filler, 1 Gallon White Enamel.
July 25.............	Wm. P. Fuller & Co	45 Gallons Boiled Oil, 3 lbs. Litharge.
July 29.............	Yates & Co	400 lbs. White Lead, 10 lbs. Tuscan Red, ½ Gallon Asphaltum Varnish.
August 1..........	Bass, Hueter & Co	10 lbs. Burnt Umber, 10 lbs. Burnt Sienna, 10 lbs. Raw Sienna, 2 Boxes ½-in. Gold Ribbon.
August 1..........	Yates & Co.	3 Gallons Shellac, 5 lbs. Indian Red.
August 2..........	Wm. P. Fuller & Co......	20 lbs. Drop Black, 6 Tubes Chrome Yellow.
August 3..........	Yates & Co.............	20 lbs. Carriage Paint, Lake.
August 4..........	Wm. P. Fuller & Co	100 lbs. Dry Metallic.

GOODS RECEIVED—Continued.

DATE.	NAME.	ARTICLES.
1898—August 12.........	Yates & Co.........................	50 Gallons Turpentine, 50 lbs. Dry White Lead.
August 13.........	Yates & Co	25 lbs. Red Lead.
August 17.........	Wm. P. Fuller & Co	30 lbs. Dark English Vermillion, 2 Gallons Body Varnish, 5 Gallons No. 1 Coach Varnish.
August 26.........	Wm. P. Fuller & Co	2 Gallons Coach Rubbing Varnish.
August 29.........	Yates & Co	5 Tubes Carmine, ½ Dozen ½-in. Flat Fitches, ½ Dozen 1½-in. Flat Fitches, ½ Dozen No. 8 King Sash Tools, 1 Dozen 1-in. Camel Hair Color Brushes, 1 Dozen 2-in. Camel Hair Color Brushes, 1 Gallon White Shellac.
August 29.........	Yat s & Co	3 Boxes ½-in. Ribbon Gold Leaf.
August 30.........	Jas. A. Snook & Co........	1 Realm No. 1 Sand Paper.
September 1....	Yates & Co	400 lbs. White Lead.
September 7....	Wm. P. Fuller & Co	50 Gallons Boiled Oil.
September 19..	Wm. P. Fuller & Co	100 lbs. Dry Metallic.
October 1...... ..	Yates & Co	¼ Gallon Orange Shellac.
October 25	Wm. P. Fuller & Co	1 Gallon Body Varnish, 1 Gallon Coach Rubbing Varnish.
November 11...	Yates & Co.....................	12 Blocks Eureka Stone, 10 lbs. Lake, 10 lbs. Aurora Red, 10 lbs. Tuscan, 20 lbs. Rough Stuff.
November 22...	Wm. P. Fuller & Co	1 Gallon Body Varnish.
December 3.....	Wm. P. Fuller & Co	2 Gallons Body Varnish, 1 Gallon Rubbing Varnish, 15 lbs. English Vermillion.

GOODS RECEIVED—Continued.

DATE.	NAME.	ARTICLES.
1898—December 6.....	Yates & Co	200 lbs White Lead, ½ Gallon Shellac.
December 10...	Yates & Co	20 Gallons Turpentine, 300 lbs. White Lead, 1 Gallon White Shellac, 1 Gallon Orange Shellac, 10 lbs. Lake Color, 10 lbs. Wine Color, 10 lbs. Tuscan Red, 10 lbs. Brunt Umber, 12 Blocks Eureka Stone, 5 Tubes Carmine, 1-3 Dozen No. 150 Putty Knives, 1-3 Dozen No. 300 Stiff Knives, 1-3 Dozen 1¼-in. Putty Knives.
December 13...	Wm. P. Fuller & Co.. ...	50 Gallons Boiled Oil, 20 Gallons Raw Oil, 1 Case Babbitts Lye, 2 Gallons Body Varnish, 2 Gallons Rubbing Varnish, 20 lbs. Drop Black, 1 lb. Lamp Black, 2 2-3 Boxes ½-in. Ribbon Gold Leaf, 3 Boxes ¾-in. Ribbon Gold Leaf, 1 Package XX Gold Leaf, 3 Gallons Ammonia, 3 Dusters, 30 lbs. Dark English Vermillion, 1-6 Dozen No. 5 Black Sable Pencils, 1-6 Dozen No. 3 Black Sable Pencils, 1-6 Dozen No. 2 Black Sable Pencils, ¼ Dozen Small Stripers, 1-12 Dozen No. 2 Lacquering Brush.
1899—January 12.......	Moise, Klinkner & Co ...	1 Pair Pads.
January 13.......	Wm. P. Fuller & Co	¼ Dozen 1½-in. Badger Brushes, 1 lb. Dry Ivory Drop Black.
January 30.......	Wm. P. Fuller & Co.......	2 Gallons Body Varnish, 1 Gallon Rubbing Varnish, 10 lbs. Light English Vermillion, 1 Box Pummice Stone.
January 30.......	Yates & Co	12 Bladders Putty.
February 5	Wm. P. Fuller & Co	1 Light Glass 18 x 22.
February 11.....	Yates & Co	300 lbs. White Lead.
February 15.....	Wm. P. Fuller & Co......	1-12 Dozen Large Bottle Gold Paint, 1 Quart White Copal Varnish, 1 Quart Dark Copal Varnish.

GOODS RECEIVED—CONTINUED.

DATE.	NAME.	ARTICLES.
1899—February 16.....	Yates & Co	10 lbs. Carriage Part Lake, 5 lbs. Aurora Red, 3 Tubes U. M. Blue.
February 16.....	Bass, Hueter & Co.........	10 lbs. Burnt Umber, 10 lbs. Burnt Sienna, 5 lbs. Raw Sienna.
March 1.........	Yates & Co......................	300 lbs. White Lead, 1 Keg Red Lead, 10 lbs. Lake, 10 lbs. Burnt Sienna.
March 1...........	Wm. P. Fuller & Co.......	50 Gallons Boiled Oil, 1 Gallon Rubbing Varnish.
March 1...........	Yates & Co......................	1 Keg Red Lead, 10 lbs. Lake Color, 25 lbs. Dry White Lead, 300 lbs. Dry White Lead.
March 6...	Snook & Co....................	1 Realm No. 1 Sand Paper, 1 Realm No. 2 Sand Paper, 1 Realm No. 3 Sand Paper.
March 22.........	Bass, Hueter & Co.........	10 lbs. Burnt Sienna.
April 4............	Yates & Co	600 lbs. White Lead, 50 Gallons Turpentine, 50 lbs. Dry White Lead, 1 Gallon White Shellac, 13 lbs. Aurora Red, 20 lbs. Lake. 10 lbs. Tuscan Red, 10 lbs. Prussian Blue, 3 Gallons Japan, 1 Dozen No. 30 O. K. Brushes, 5 lbs. Lamp Black, 8 Tubes Carmine, 5 lbs. Lump Pummice, 75 lbs. Litharge, ½ Gallon Black Asphaltum.
April 4...........	Bass, Hueter & Co.........	10 lbs. Burnt Sienna, 10 lbs. Raw Sienna, 10 lbs. Burnt Umber, 10 lbs. Raw Umber.
April 7............	Wm. P. Fuller & Co	50 Gallons Boiled Oil, 50 Gallons Raw Oil, 100 lbs. Dry Metallic, 12 Bladders Putty, 5 Gallons Body Varnish, 3 Gallons Rubbing Varnish, 3 Gallons No. 1 Coach Varnish, 30 lbs. Ivory Black, 25 lbs. Zinc, 30 lbs. English Vermillion, ½ Dozen 1½-in. Badger Brushes, 3 Boxes ½-in. Ribbon Gold Leaf, 3 Boxes ¾-in. Ribbon Gold Leaf, 1 Package Gold Leaf, ¼ Dozen Yellow Lake, ½ Dozen Flake White, ¼ Dozen Naples Yellow, 1 Gallon Japan Gold Size, ¼ Dozen Tubes Verdigris.

GOODS RECEIVED—Continued.

DATE.	NAME.	ARTICLES.
1899—April 12............	Wm. P. Fuller & Co	6 Tubes Flake White, 1 lb. Naples Yellow.
April 12............	Bass, Hueter & Co.........	1 Brush Can Holder.
April 14............	Wm. P. Fuller & Co	1-3 Dozen 2-in. Varnish Brushes, 1-12 Dozen 1½-in. Varnish Brushes, 1-3 Dozen C. H. Lachie Brushes, ½ Dozen C. H. Asst. Super. Brushes, 1 Box Crayons, ½ Dozen ½ Camel Hair Pencils, 1-12 Dozen 2-in. Black and Tan Brush.
April 23............	Yates & Co	1 Gallon White Enamel.
May 2............		800 lbs. White Lead, 15 lbs. Lamp Black, 5 lbs. Venetian Red, 3 lbs. Alum, 2 lbs. White Glue, 25 lbs. Flour.
May 2............	Corporation Yard No. 1.	1 Gallon Alcohol.
May 2............	John Quadt..................	80 Rolls Wall Paper, 10 Rolls Border Paper, 70 Rolls Ceiling Paper, 10 Rolls Decoration Paper, 2 Sets Corners, 12 Rolls Ingrain.
May 4............	Wm. P. Fuller & Co	10 lbs. Plaster Paris, 1 Bottle Burnt Sienna W. Color, 1 Bottle Burnt Umber W. Color, 1 Bottle Raw Sienna, W. Color, 1 Bottle Chrome Yellow W. Color, 10 lbs. Paris White.
May 8............	Yates & Co	24-30 O. K. Flat Paint Brushes.
May 15............	Wm. P. Fuller & Co	50 Gallons Boiled Oil, 1-3 Dozen No. 30 Elastic Putty Knives, 1-3 Dozen No. 30 Stiff Putty Knives, 1-3 Dozen No. 130-1½ Putty Knives, ½ Dozen ½ Flat Fitches, ½ Dozen 1½ Flat Fitches, ½ Dozen No. 8 Sash Tools.
May 18............	Corporation Yard No. 1.	1 Dozen Large Paint Pots, 1 Dozen Small Paint Pots.

GOODS RECEIVED—Continued.

DATE.	NAME.	ARTICLES.
1899—May 26	Wm. P. Fuller & Co	1 Dozen Bottles Ammonia, 5 lbs. Blueing. 4 S. C. Badger Brushes No. 1, 4 S. C. Badger Brushes No. 2.
June 5	Wm. P. Fuller & Co	2 Gallons No. 1 Coach Varnish, 10 lbs. Venetian Red.
June 7	Wm. P. Fuller & Co	1 Gallon White Shellac.
June 10	Wm. P. Fuller & Co	50 Gallons Boiled Oil.
June 10	Yates & Co	1000 lbs. White Lead, 10 lbs. Carriage, Part Lake.
June 20	Wm. P. Fuller & Co	200 lbs. Dry Metallic.

GOODS DELIVERED FROM JULY 1, 1898, TO JULY 1, 1899.

DATE.	DEPARTMENT.	Order	ARTICLES.
898—July 6...............	Corporation Yard No. 1		5 lbs. Lake Varnish Color, 5 lbs Vermillion Varnish Color, ½ Gallon Rubbing Varnish.
July 6......	Plumbing Department.	664	3 Bladders Putty.
July 8...............	Engine No. 19...............	665	5 lbs. White Enamel Paint.
July 9	Carpenter Shop...........	662	10 Gallons Raw Linseed Oil.
July 9...............	Engine No. 34...............	668	2½ Gallons Mixed Paint, 1 lb. Burnt Sienna, 24 Sheets Sand Paper, 2 lbs. Putty.
July 11...............	Engine No. 2...............	695	3 Tubes Vertigrease, 3 Rolls ½-in. Gold Ribbon, 3 Rolls ¾-in. Gold Ribbon, 1 1-in. Fitch Tool, 1 1½-in. Burnisher, 14 oz. Gold Lachle, 1 1½-in. Flat Brush.
July 11...............	Hydrantmen Department	674	1 Flat Brush.
July 16...............	Engine No. 24...............	677	8 Gallons Boiled Oil.
July 16...............	Corporation Yard No. 1		1 Pint Varnish.
July 22...............	Corporation Yard No. 1		1 Quart Varnish.
July 23...............	Engine No. 1......	684	1 Flat Brush.
July 23...............	Truck No. 3...............	686	½ Gallon Boiled Oil.
July 25...............	Carpenter shop............	686	10 Gallons Raw Linseed Oil.
July 25...............	Corporation Yard No. 1		3 lbs. Litharge.
July 26...............	Hydrantmen Department	689	10 Gallons Mixed Paint.
July 30.	Plumbing Department	694	7 Gallons Boiled Oil.
August 1........	Engine No. 27...............	696	5 lbs. Indian Red, 3 lbs. Drop Black, 2 lbs. Burnt Umber, 1 lb. Chrome Yellow, 2 Gallons Turpentine, 3 Gallons Orange Shellac, 1 Gallon Alcohol.

GOODS DELIVERED—CONTINUED.

DATE.	DEPARTMENT.	Order ...	ARTICLES.
1899—August 1........	Engine No. 10...............	608	60 lbs. White Lead, 3 Gallons Boiled Oil, 1 Gallon Turpentine, ½ Bladder Putty, 2 lbs. Lamp Black, 5 lbs. Yellow Ochre, 2 lbs. Tuscan Red, 1 lb. Burnt Sienna, 1 Quart No. 1 Coach Varnish, 1 Sash Tool.
August 4..........	Plumbing Department	607	10 Gallons Boiled Oil, 100 lbs. Dry Metallic.
August 10........	Engine No. 3...............	701	2 Gallons Boiled Oil.
August 10.........	Engine No. 11..............	701	15 Gallons Mixed Paint, 3 Paint Pots, 3 Flat Brushes.
August 12.........	Truck No. 1....................	702	50 lbs. White Lead, 3 Gallons Boiled Oil, 2 Gallons Turpentine, 1 Gallon Varnish, 5 lbs. Burnt Umber, 4 lbs. Burnt Sienna, 3 lbs. Chrome Yellow, 2 lbs. Raw Sienna, 1 lb. Putty, 6 Sheets Sand Paper, 1 Pint Japan, 5 lbs. Zinc, 1 Flat Brush, 1 Sash Tool, 1 Whitewash Brush.
August 13.........	Engine No. 15...............	705	¾ Gallons White Paint, ¾ Gallons White Enamel.
August 20...	Corporation Yard No. 1		2 lbs. Lake Color, 3 lbs. Vermillion, 1 Quart Varnish.
August 21.........	Corporation Yard.........		New Ladders, 1 Gallon Mixed Paint.
August 29.........	Engine No. 7..................	708	1 Gallon White Shellac, 1 Gallon Alcohol.
August 29.........	Engine No. 11...................	712	10 Gallons Mixed Paint.
September 2....	Carpenter Shop............	715	1½ Gallons Mixed Paint.
September 7....	Engine No. 11...............	715	10 Gallons Mixed Paint, 10 Gallons Boiled Oil, 1 Gallon Turpentine.
September 7....	Engine No. 2.................	713	½ Gallon Raw Linseed Oil.
September 8....	Chemical No. 5..............	718	2 Gallons Floor Paint.
September 10..	Chemical No. 5..............	718	3 Gallons Mixed Paint.

GOODS DELIVERED—Continued.

DATE.	DEPARTMENT.	Order	ARTICLES.
808—September 15..	Engine No. 28............	720	7 Gallons Roofing Paint.
September 15..	Engine No. 11............	720	3 Gallons Boiled Oil.
October 18	Chemical No. 5............	726	3 Gallons Mixed Paint, ½ Gallon Boiled Oil, ½ Gallon Turpentine, 3 Quarts Varnish.
October 18.......	Corporation Yard No.1		2 lbs. Lake Color, 2 lbs. Vermillion, 1 Quart Varnish.
October 31	Chemical No. 5............	735	1 Gallon Roofing Paint.
November 2...	Engine No. 2............	729	1 Gallon Mixed Paint.
November 10...	Harness Department...	731	1 Gallon Turpentine, ½ Gallon Varnish, 1 lb. Drop Black.
November 19...	Truck No. 2............	735	1½ Gallon Paint.
November 26...	Carpenter Shop............	....	1 Gallon Priming Color.
December 7.....	Engine No. 35............	741	15 Gallons Boiled Oil, 1 Paint Brush, 1 lb. Burnt Umber.
December 13...	Corporation Yard No.1		1 Package Lamp Black, 1 Gallon Turpentine.
December 13...	Hydrantmen Department..	744	10 Gallons Mixed Paint.
December 14...	Corporation Yard No.1		2 Bladders Putty.
December 16...	Chemical No. 5............	764	1½ Gallons Mixed Paint.
December 17...	Corporation Yard No.1		1 Quart Lake Varnish Color.
1899—January 6........	Engine No. 25............	752	10 Gallons Boiled Oil, 2 lbs. Burnt Umber.
January 12.......	Truck No. 3..	754	½ Gallon Cherry Stain.
January 17.......	Chemical No. 4............	754	10 Gallons Mixed Paint.
January 30.......	Plumbing Department	764	5 Gallons Boiled Oil, 1 Bladder Putty.

GOODS DELIVERED—Continued.

DATE.	DEPARTMENT.	Order	ARTICLES.
1899—January 31	Corporation Yard No.1		2 lbs. Lake Color, 1 lb. Vermillion, 1 Quart Varnish.
February 5	Corporation Yard No.2		1 Light Glass 18 x 22.
February 9	Engine No. 1	784	4 Gallons Mixed Paint, 1 Bladder Putty.
February 10	Chemical No. 4	768	10 Gallons Boiled Oil, 2 lbs. Burnt Umber.
February 10	Hydrantmen Department	767	10 Gallons Mixed Paint.
February 16	Engine No. 1	784	4 Gallons Mixed Paint.
February 18	Corporation Yard No.1		3 Pints Varnish, 3 lbs. Lake Color.
February 24	Engine No. 1	784	3 Gallons Mixed Paint.
March 1	Chemical No. 4	778	7 Gallons Mixed Paint, 3 Gallons Boiled Oil, 1 Bladder Putty.
March 1	Engine No. 30	778	1 Quart Lead Color, 1 lb. Burnt Sienna, 1 Gallon Turpentine, 1 Quart Varnish.
March 1	Engine No. 1	784	9 Gallons Mixed Paint.
March 7	Engine No. 2	783	2 Gallons Raw Linseed Oil.
March 7	Corporation Yard No.1		2 Paint Brushes, 1 Paint Pot.
March 15	Corporation Yard No.1		2 lbs. Lake Color, 4 lbs. Vermillion, 3 Pints Varnish.
March 17	Plumbing Department	787	3 Bladders Putty.
March 25	Water Tower No. 2	791	1 Pint Mixed Paint.
March 26	Truck No. 4	789	2 Gallons Mixed Paint.
March 30	Engine No. 1	792	3 Gallons Mixed Paint.
April 7	Chemical No. 2	801	10 Gallons Boiled Oil, 1 lb. Burnt Umber.

GOODS DELIVERED—CONTINUED.

DATE.	DEPARTMENT.	Order	ARTICLES.
39—April 7........, ...	Truck No. 2.	784	½ Gallon Mixed Paint.
April 10............	Corporation Yard No. 1	....	2 Bladders Putty, 4 lbs. Lake Color, 3 lbs. Vermillion, 1 lb. Burnt Sienna, 1 Gallon Boiled Oil.
April 15	Engine No. 14	802	2 Gallons White Shellac, 1 Gallon Alcohol.
April 15............	Chemical No. 5............	784	½ Gallon Mixed Paint.
April 19............	Corporation Yard No. 1	....	2 lbs. Lake Color, 3 lbs. Vermillion.
April 20............	Corporation Yard No. 2	....	2 Dozen Sheets Sand Paper, 4 Gallons Paint.
April 20............	Carpenter Shop............	803	3 Flat Brushes.
April 27	Corporation Yard No. 1	....	1 lb. Drop Black.
April 25............	Engine No. 21...............	805	1 Gallon Mixed Paint, ½ Gallon Bath Tub Enamel, 24 Sheets Sand Paper, 2 1-in. Brushes.
April 29............	Corporation Yard No. 1	....	1 Flat Fitch Brush.
May 4...	Engine No. 20............ ...	813	15 Gallons Boiled Oil, 2 lbs. Burnt Umber.
May 4...............	Engine No. 17................	813	6 Gallons Mixed Paint.
May 26............	Engine No. 17................	824	1 Pint Black Paint.
May 29............	Corporation Yard No. 1	....	3 lbs. Vermillion, 1 lb. Drop Black, 1 Quart Varnish, 2 lbs. Lake Color.
May 31............	Engine No. 20................	828	300 lbs. White Lead, 11 Gallons Boiled Oil, 7 Gallons Turpentine, 1½ Bladders Putty, 1 Pint Varnish, 3 lbs. Raw Sienna, 4 lbs. Burnt Sienna, 3 lbs. Burnt Umber, 1 lb Chrome Yellow, 1 lb. Drop Black, 5 Gallons Mixed Paint.

GOODS DELIVERED—CONTINUED.

DATE.	DEPARTMENT.	Order.	ARTICLES.
1899—June 5..........	Corporation Yard Woodworker..............	....	5 Quires Sand Paper.
June 5..............	Harness Department...	823	1 Gallon Turpentine, 1 Gallon Varnish, 1 lb. Drop Black.
June 9..............	Corporation Yard No. 1	....	1 Gallon Mixed Paint, 1 Brush, 25 lbs. Red Lead.
June 19.............	Corporation Yard Annex	....	1 Brush for Dynamo, 4 Gallons Boiled Oil, 3 Papers Lamp Black.
June 20.............	Corporation Yard No. 1	....	2 lbs. Vermillion, 1 Pint Varnish.
June 20.......	Plumbing Department	831	5 Gallons Boiled Oil, 100 lbs. Metallic.
June 25.......	Engine No. 14.......	835	400 lbs. White Lead, 15 Gallons Boiled Oil, 15 Gallons Turpentine, 8 lbs. Raw Sienna, 6 lbs. Burnt Sienna, 6 lbs. Burnt Umber, 1 lb. Drop Black, 2 lbs. Chrome Yellow. 1 Quart Japan, 1 Pint Varnish, 2 Gallons Varnish.
June 26.	Stable Annex	834	11 Gallons Mixed Paint, 1 Gallon Boiled Oil, 1 Gallon Turpentine, 1 lb. Burnt Sienna, 1 Quart Varnish, 1 Quart Turpentine, ½ Gallon Gasoline.
June 26.............	Corporation Yard No. 2, Annex, Engine No. 28. Tower..	836	1000 lbs. White Lead, 65 Gallons Boiled Oil, 30 Gallons Turpentine, 5 lbs. Plaster Paris, 4 Bottles Water Colors, 10 lbs. Paris White, 20 lbs. Lamp Black, 10 lbs. Venetian Red, 3 lbs. Alum, 2 lbs. Glue, 25 lbs. Flour, 2 Bladders Putty, 2 lbs. Chrome Yellow, 1 Quart Japan, 1 lb. Burnt Sienna, 1 lb. Umber, 1 lb. Tuscan Red, 1 lb. Prussian Blue, 31 lbs. Mixed Paint, 150 lbs. Metallic.

Yours respectfully,

CHAS. F. HEALEY,
Department Painter.

REPORT OF DEPARTMENT HARNESSMAKER.

SAN FRANCISCO, July 1, 1899.

To the Honorable the Board of Fire Commissioners and the Chief Engineer—

Gentlemen: I herewith submit the Annual Report of the Harness Shop, with an account of all new work, repairs, stock on hand, etc., ending June 30, 1899:
This shop has made during the year—

Bridles, extra, new style	49
Bridles, Pigeon-wing, team	12
Breeching bodies, extra	8
Breeching straps, extra pairs	12
Back and Hip straps, extra pairs	2
Breast straps, extra pairs, team	2
Buggy reins, extra pairs	5
Buggy breastplates, extra	3
Buggy body girths, extra	6
Buggy crupper docks, extra	1
Braiding crackers on straight and bow whips	103
Cushions, curled hair, buggy	6
Cushions, restuffing buggy and cart	5
Covering buggy and cart dash boards	8
Covering buggy and cart lazy backs	4
Covering buggy boots	2
Covering ladder stands for hose wagons	24
Covering ladder carries for trucks	17
Covering pairs of pole chains	11
Cheeks, pairs of square blind buggy	4
Cross check reins	8
Cart saddle for battery, 7 inches	1
Canvas outside hose wagon covers for Wagons Nos. 4, 45, 46 and 47	4
Canvas go between hose wagon covers	5
Canvas dash and lap covers, lined with blanket for officers' buggies	3
Canvas drop aprons	3
Canvas bags for 3 Way Siamese connections	13
Canvas bags for gloves	71
Canvas bags for wire cutters	28
Canvas bags for circulating nozzles	20
Dozen straps of assorted sizes	119
Dozen leather washers, assorted, for suctions, nozzles and hose couplings	141½
Dozen rubber gasket, assorted, for hydrants	46½
Enameled duck curtain	1
Fitting Hale's patent forged hames to new collars	14
Horse blankets, 7 ft. covered with 40-inch canvas	20
Horse blankets repaired	35
Horse boots, shin and ankle with 24-inch elastic	4
Horse boots, ankle with 10-inch elastic	2
Horse boot cornet	2
Horse boots, repaired shin and ankle with 24-inch elastic	5

Horse boots, repaired ankle with 10-inch elastic.............................. 10
Horse boots, repaired knee... 4
Horse and ladder straps... 62
Hold backs, pairs, 2-inch.. 2
Hobbles, leather... 2
Handle on 3 Way Siamese connection.. 17
Leather book cases, to hold books showing size of water mains and receipt
    books 9
Leather boxes for smoke muzzles... 6
Leather smoke muzzles... 12
Leather boxes for small life line... 6
Leather boxes for gun cartridges.. 2
Leather ceiling hook cases.. 11
Leather whip sockets.. 4
Nozzle boxes for 2½ inch shut off nozzles....................................... 0
Nozzle boxes for 3-inch controlling nozzle with 14-inch elastic................. 22
Nozzle tip covers, leather.. 40
Oiling new canvas outside hose wagon covers..................................... 5
Oiling new canvas go between hose wagon covers.................................. 5
Oiling new canvas dash and lap covers... 3
Oiling new canvas engine apron, Engine 19....................................... 1
Repairing, washing, blacking and oiling sets of buggy harness................... 17
Repairing, washing, blacking and oiling sets of team harness.................... 7
Sets of double team harness... 15
Sets of single buggy harness.. 3
Sets of single spring wagon harness... 1
Sets of single battery harness.. 2
Sets of two-horse reins, extra.. 1
Sets of three-horse reins, extra.. 1
Shaft tugs, pairs... 7
Shaft straps for three-horse hitch.. 12
Spike covers with 8-inch of elastic... 16
Suction leathers, assorted.. 50
Saw cases, leather.. 2
Stuffed gig housings.. 5
Strap horse muzzles... 3
Trimming officers' buggies, complete.. 3

We have repaired more or less the harness for the whole Department. These repairs were made on harness used by officers' engines, hose wagons, chemical engines, trucks, water tower, batteries, hydrantman, harnessmaker, carpenter's buggy and lumber wagon, plumber, teamser's and department stables.

We have also repaired:

Hale's patent forged hames and collars.. 3
Hale's patent angle iron hames and collars...................................... 12
Hale's patent buggy forged hames and collar..................................... 1
Berry's patent hames and collars.. 26

The Harness in use consists of:

Sets of double in engine companies.. 84
Sets of double in relief engine companies Nos. 1, 4 and 5....................... 5½
Sets of double in chemical engine companies..................................... 7
Sets of double in relief chemical engines company............................... 1
Sets of double in truck companies... 10½
Sets of double in Water Tower... 1½
Sets of double in Coal Supply Wagon No. 2....................................... 1½
Sets of double in Department Stable... 3
Sets of double for teamsters at Corporation Yard No. 1.......................... 3

Sets of double for carpenter's lumber wagon.................................... 1
Sets of single, cart for Battery.................................... 2
Sets of single, buggy for Officers.................................... 12
Sets of single, buggy for Hydrantman.................................... 6
Sets of single, buggy for harnessmaker.................................... 1
Sets of single, buggy for carpenter.................................... 1
Sets of single, buggy for drayman and stable.................................... 2
Sets of single for delivery wagon at stable.................................... 1
Sets of single for delivery wagon at Corporation Yard No. 1.................. 1
Sets of single for delivery wagon at Corporation Yard No. 2.................. 1
Sets of single for plumber's wagon.................................... 1

Hames and Collars in use consists of:
Hale's patent old style forged hames and collars.................................... 11
Hale's patent new style forged hames and collars.................................... 112
Hale's patent angle iron hames and collars.................................... 37
Berry's patent hames and collars.................................... 62
Armstrong's patent single hames and collar for battery.................... 1
Odd single hames and collar for battery.................................... 1
Hale's patent forged single hames and collars for buggy.................... 1
Berry's patent hames and collars for buggy.................................... 5
Express collar and hames for plumber.................................... 1
Express collar and hames for Department stable.................... 1
Boston team collars and hames for teamsters and stables.................... 14

The Harness in Reserve consists of:
Sets of double for companies and teamsters.................................... 20½
Sets of single, cart for batteries.................................... 2

Hames and Collars in Reserve consists of:
Hale's patent old style forged hames and collars.................................... 1
Hale's patent new style forged hames and collars.................................... 23
Hale's patent angle iron hames and collars.................................... 6
Berry's patent hames and collars.................................... 19
Hale's patent extension hames and collars for buggy.................... 3
Berry's patent hames and collars for buggy.................................... 2
Boston team collars, for teamsters and stable.................... 10
Pairs No. 8 x. c. bolt hames for teamsters and stable...................... 12

All Engines, Trucks, Water Tower, Relief Engine No. 5 and Coal Supply Wagon
No. 2, have 3-horse hitch, except Engines Nos 6 and 9.

Delivered to Fire Alarm and Police Telegraph:
One set double team harness, complete with Boston team collars and No. 8
x. c. bolt hames.

New Stock on Hand:
Hale's patent new style forged hames, not fitted to collars.................... 8
New horse collars without hames, for Hale's patent forged hames............ 12

Stock on hand:
Bits on hand July 1, 1898.................................... 74
Bits received from July 1, 1898, to June 30, 1899........................ 186
Bits delivered from July 1, 1898 to June 30, 1899........................170
Bits on hand July 1, 1899.................................... 90
                                                        ———   ———
                                                        260   260

```
Straight whips on hand July 1, 1898.....................................     23
Straight whips received from July 1, 1898, to June 30, 1899............     24
Straight whips delivered from July 1, 1898, to June 30, 1899.......... 29
Straight whips on hand July 1, 1899..................................... 18
                                                                       ──    ──
                                                                       47    47

Bow whips on hand July 1, 1898...........................................     30
Bow whips received from July 1, 1898, to June 30, 1899................     36
Bow whips delivered from July 1, 1898, to June 30, 1899.............. 51
Bow whips on hand July 1, 1899........................................ 15
                                                                       ──    ──
                                                                       66    66

Armstrong snaps on hand July 1, 1898.................................     31
Armstrong snaps received from July 1, 1898, to June 30, 1899.........     12
Armstrong snaps delivered from July 1, 1898, to June 30, 1899........ 24
Armstrong snaps on hand July 1, 1899................................. 22
                                                                       ──    ──
                                                                       46    46

Blankets on hand July 1, 1898...........................................     53
Blankets received from July 1, 1898, to June 30, 1899.....................     20
Blankets delivered from July 1, 1898, to June 30, 1899.................. 29
Blankets on hand July 1, 1899............................................. 44
                                                                       ──    ──
                                                                       73    73
```

In every company there is one extra bridle and bit.

The harness, bits, blankets, through the Department are all in first-class condition.

Respectfully submitted,

I. GURMENDEZ,
Foreman Harness Maker.

REPORT OF VETERINARY SURGEON.

San Francisco, July 1st, 1899.

To the Honorable the Board of Fire Commissioners and the Chief Engineer—

Gentlemen: I hereby submit my Annual Report:

There are at present in service in the Department 292 horses, including those kept for relief.

With exception of 18 that are now under treatment at the hospital for various ailments, and five that are being treated at the engine houses for minor troubles, that do not necessitate their being put out of service, they are all in good condition.

During the year 39 horses were purchased, 29 condemned as being unfit for service, 23 of which were sold at public auction, the remaining 6 being transferred to Branch County Jail No. 2, by order of the Board of Supervisors.

Six horses were shot for broken legs, one for injured spine, and six died from sickness at the hospital, making a total of 13 deaths during the year.

Four hundred and twenty-three cases of sickness or injury have been treated at the hospital, and 186 cases in the engine houses, without taking them out of service.

There are at present 18 on the hospital sick list, and 5 being treated in the engine houses.

All of the horses have had their teeth attended to.

I have visited the hospital at least once a day, and the engine houses once a month, besides attending to the calls to sick horses.

Besides the 292 horses mentioned above there are three colts, making a total of 295.   Respectfully submitted,

WILLIAM F. EGAN, M. R. C. V. S.,
Veterinary Surgeon to the Department.

4

REPORT OF DEPARTMENT PLUMBER.

San Francisco, July 1, 1899.

To the Honorable the Board of Fire Commissioners and the Chief Engineer—

Gentlemen: I herewith present my Report as Department Plumber for Fiscal Year ending June 30, 1899:

Engine House No. 1—Fitted up new sink in yard; run cast-iron sewer to rear shed; repaired bath tub, basin and water closet; made gas and water pipe extensions.

Engine House No. 2—Repaired wash basin and water closet; put in new urinal; run new waste from urinal to sewer; made gas and water pipe extensions.

Engine House No. 3—Repaired break in sewer; changed rear stall waste; reset slop-hopper fitted up grain-steamer in yard; changed water-pipe and repaired gas pipe.

Engine House No. 4—Fitted up new enamel sink; lined water closet tank; put in new basin cock; reset wash basin, repaired stall wastes.

Engine House No. 7—Run new waste from sink to sewer; put new trap under sink; changed water pipe; repaired sink, bath and basin faucets.

Engine House No. 8—Cleared and repaired sewer; put new strainers on all stall wastes; repaired sink and urinal wastes.

Engine House No. 10—Put in new stall wastes; repaired water closet and sink; run water and gas pipes.

Engine House No. 11—Put entire new plumbing throughout building; gas and water; soil waste and vent pipes; two syphon water closets; enameled bath-tub, wash basin; marble slab sink and slop hopper; hot water boiler and supply tank on roof.

Engine House No. 13—Put in new bath-tub and water closet; changed urinal from inside to outside of building; run gas and water waste and vent pipes.

Engine House No. 14—Repaired water closets on first and second floors; also, repaired bath, basin and urinal.

Engine House No. 15—Put in new basin cock; repaired water closet; run gas and water pipe.

Engine House No. 16—Put in gas and water pipe; repaired water closet, bath and basin; also, stall wastes.

Engine House No. 17—Repaired sink and urinal; made gas and water pipe extensions; also, changed stair rail.

Engine House No. 18—Repaired stall wastes; also, repaired water closet, sink, bath and basin faucets.

Engine No. 19 (Old House)—Changed gas and water pipes; repaired water closet and gas fixtures.

Engine House No. 20—Put in new stall wastes; also, new sink and urinal, new syphon; changed gas and water pipes.

Engine House No. 22—Put in new stall wastes; repaired urinal; made gas pipe extensions.

Engine House No. 23—Run new wastes from sink and urinal; put new traps under same; changed water and vent pipes.

Engine House No. 24—Put in new stall wastes; run cast-iron sewer connections; also, made gas and water pipe extensions; put new trap under sink.

Engine House No. 25—Changed all stall wastes; made gas and water pipe extensions; repaired water closet; put tank on roof to supply hot water boiler.

Engine House No. 31—Cleared and repaired sewer, put new trap under sink; repaired urinal and rear stall wastes.

Engine No. 32 (New House)—Repaired water closets; put in new faucets.

Engine House No. 33—Put in new marble slab and wash bowl; new trap under same; repaired water closet and stall wastes; put new strainers on all stall wastes.

Truck No. 1—Repaired sewer; put in three new sections; repaired sink, urinal and basin wastes; also, repaired stall wastes.

Truck No. 3—Put in new syphon water closet bowl; cleared sink, urinal and stall wastes; made gas pipe extensions.

Truck No. 7—Repaired wash-basin and bath-tub; cleared and repaired gas pipe and fixtures.

Chemical No. 2 (New House), Sunset District—Fitted up tank in hose tower to supply hot water boiler; made gas and water pipe extensions.

Chemical No. 4—Put in new cast-iron sewer, gas, water, soil, waste and vent pipes, new sink and urinal, new stall wastes and slop-hopper; changed bath, basin and water closet and tank on roof, and boiler from main building to new addition; also, run gas and sewer pipes to rear shed.

New Drill Tower (Rear of No. 28 Engine House)—Fitted up room with gas and water pipes, two enameled sinks, cast-iron sewer, waste and leader pipes.

Engine House No. 28 (Annex)—Fitted up one story building with gas and water pipes, cast-iron sewer and leader pipes; run wastes from five stalls.

Department Stables—Made and put up new gas fixtures; run new wastes, and changed supply pipes to front and rear drinking troughs.

Corporation Yard No. 1—Put in urinal on second floor, urinal taken from No. 2 Engine House; repaired water closet; made gas pipe extensions.

Corporation Yard No. 2—Put in new sink and urinal; run gas and water pipes; also waste and vent pipes.

Also repaired plumbing at various times through the year in the following houses:

Engine Houses Nos. 1, 2, 3, 4, 7, 8, 10, 11, 13, 14, 15, 16, 17, 18, 20, 21, 22, 23, 24, 25, 26, 27, 30, 31, 32, 33, 34.

Truck Houses 1, 2, 3 and 7.

Chemical Houses 2, 3 and 4.

Corporation Yards 1 and 2.

Department Stables.

Plumbing Material on hand June 30, 1899.

Three 53-gallon galvanized iron boilers; 4 sheets zinc; 12 1-swing gas brackets; 12 2-swing gas brackets; 36 ¾-inch hose cocks; 200 lbs. caulking lead; 24 4-inch brass strainers; 50 lbs. wiping solder; 800 ft. galvanized iron water pipe; 700 ft. gas pipe; about 300 lbs. of gas and water pipe fittings; 150 ft. 4-inch cast-iron pipe; 60 4-inch cast-iron fittings; 130 ft. 3-inch cast-iron pipe; 70 3-inch cast-iron fittings; 200 ft. 2-inch cast-iron pipe; 90 2-inch cast-iron fittings.

Respectfully submitted,

JAMES BYRNE,

Department Plumber.

OFFICERS, MEMBERS AND EMPLOYEES

OF THE

SAN FRANCISCO FIRE DEPARTMENT.

D. T. SULLIVAN....................................Chief Engineer

JOHN DOUGHERTY...................Assistant Chief Engineer

T. M. FERNANDEZ..........................Assistant Engineer

P. H. SHAUGHNESSY........................Assistant Engineer

JOHN WILLS..............................Assistant Engineer

MICHAEL J. DOLAN........................Assistant Engineer

EDWARD F. McKITTRICK........Engineer Relief Engine No. 1

J. J. CONLON.....................Engineer Relief Engine No. 2

WILLIAM WALTERS............Engineer Relief Engine No. 3

JOHN McCLUSKEY...............Engineer Relief Engine No. 4

CORPORATION YARD EMPLOYEES.

JOHN W. REILLY...Superintendent of Engines

JOHN KENNEY.....................................Assistant Superintendent of Engines

HENRY H. GORTER...Machinist

P. H. FLEMING..........................Clerk and Storekeeper of Corporation Yard

PHILIP BRADY..Hydrantman

HENRY RICE...Hydrantman

ROBERT HARRIS...Drayman

JOSEPH SAWYER..Watchman

WILLIAM H. AYERS ....Carpenter

WILLIAM F. EGAN..Veterinary Surgeon

ENGINE COMPANY No. 1.

Location—No. 419 Pacific street.

NAMES.	RANK.	NO. BADGE.
Thomas Kelly	Engineer.	24
Daniel Farren	Driver.	25
C. Ward	Fireman.	26
MEMBERS AT CALL.		
Joseph Keane	Foreman.	23
Charles Schemel	Assistant Foreman.	33
J. J. Murray	Hoseman.	27
Thomas Coleman	"	28
August Banker	"	29
David Capelli	"	30
Silvia Rocco	"	31
Charles Tyson	"	32
William C Higgins	"	34

ENGINE COMPANY No. 2.

Location—No. 410 Bush street.

NAMES.	RANK.	NO. BADGE.
Charles Murray	Engineer.	36
John Johnson	Driver.	37
F. B. Dougherty	Fireman.	38
MEMBERS AT CALL		
Michael Boden	Foreman.	35
Joseph O'Brien	Assistant Foreman.	41
Thomas Muldowney	Hoseman.	39
John Leckie	"	40
Matthew McLaughlin	"	42
Charles Gallatin	"	43
E. L. Raffestin	"	44
Geo. Spellman	"	45
G. W. Dinan	"	46

ENGINE COMPANY No. 3.

Location—No. 1317 California street.

NAMES.	RANK.	NO. BADGE.
Thomas J. Canavan	Engineer.	48
Daniel Lyons	Driver.	49
William Byrnes	Fireman.	50
MEMBERS AT CALL.		
Thomas Magner	Foreman.	47
Benjamin Currier	Assistant Foreman	58
John Rudden	Hoseman	51
H. G. Root	"	52
Frank Page	"	53
S. S. Powell	"	54
John Finnigan	"	55
Uriah Graff	"	56
Walter Cline	"	57

ENGINE COMPANY No. 4.

Location—No. 144 Second street.

NAMES.	RANK.	NO. BADGE.
Michael O'Connell	Engineer.	60
Joseph Stevens	Driver.	61
Edward Lennon	Fireman.	62
MEMBERS AT CALL.		
John Wilson	Foreman.	59
N. N. Mathewson	Assistant Foreman	68
F. H. Kenny	Hoseman.	63
Edward Downes	"	64
Fred Orr	"	65
Frank Spellman	"	66
Henry Darr	"	67
Charles Dakin	"	69
B. Donnelly	"	70

ENGINE COMPANY No. 5.

Location—No.1219 Stockton street.

NAMES.	RANK.	NO. BADGE.
Thomas Coogan	Engineer.	72
Robert Malburg	Driver.	73
W. W. Harvey	Fireman.	74
MEMBERS AT CALL.		
John J. Mahoney	Foreman.	71
Daniel O'Connor	Assistant Foreman.	77
Abe Isaacs	Hoseman.	75
W. F. Gernandt	"	76
Felix Desmond	"	78
David Harrison	"	79
Matt J. Glennan	"	80
W. J. Spinetti	"	81
William Murray	"	82

ENGINE COMPANY No. 6.

Location—No. 311 Sixth street.

NAMES.	RANK.	NO. BADGE.
Patrick H. Brandon	Engineer.	84
Joseph McDonald	Driver.	85
Charles Neil	Fireman.	86
MEMBERS AT CALL.		
J. H. Hogan	Foreman.	83
Charles Cullen	Assistant Foreman.	93
Charles Steiglitz	Hoseman.	87
Thomas Parker	"	88
Joseph Bailey	"	89
Patrick Sullivan	"	90
John Titus	"	91
Edward Daunet	"	94

ENGINE COMPANY No. 7.

Location—No. 3160 Sixteenth street.

NAMES.	RANK.	NO. BADGE
Milton Morgan	Engineer.	96
Lem Rudolph	Driver.	97
J. Allen	Fireman.	98
MEMBERS AT CALL.		
Arthur Welch	Foreman.	95
Samuel E. Kennard	Assistant Foreman.	105
George Styles	Hoseman.	99
Harry Allen	"	100
Eugene McCarthy	"	101
Edward Church	"	102
Chas. Malloy.	"	103
M. Golden	"	104
E. R. Dougherty	"	106

ENGINE COMPANY No. 8.

Location—No. 1648 Pacific avenue.

NAMES.	RANK.	NO. BADGE.
Edward Colligan	Engineer.	108
D. F. Buckley	Driver.	109
A. Davis	Fireman.	110
MEMBERS AT CALL.		
Stephen Russell	Foreman.	107
Walter W. Willis	Assistant Foreman.	115
Thos. D. O'Brien	Hoseman.	111
Robert McShane	"	112
D. McAuliffe	"	113
Stephen Balk	"	114
Mathew Brown	"	116
Daniel Coughlin	"	117
L. H. Richards	"	118

ENGINE COMPANY No. 9.

Location—No. 320 Main street.

NAMES.	RANK.	NO. BADGE
J. C. Thompson	Engineer.	120
Julius B. Cane	Driver.	121
Charles Claveau	Fireman.	122
MEMBERS AT CALL.		
John Conroy	Foreman.	119
Daniel Kelly	Assistant Foreman.	126
James Bridgewood	Hoseman.	123
Geo. F. Wells	"	124
Charles Leter	"	125
Joseph Dolan	"	127
Joseph E. Paille	"	128
Louis Walters	"	129
Walter D. Conroy	"	130

ENGINE COMPANY No. 10.

Location—No. 516 Bryant street.

NAMES.	RANK.	NO. BADGE.
F. H. Sharon	Engineer.	132
James Cronin	Driver.	133
P. O'Connell	Fireman.	124
MEMBERS AT CALL.		
William Danaby	Foreman.	131
William Gill	Assistant Foreman.	135
Charles E. Durning	Hoseman	136
James McGibben	"	137
Joseph Ryan	"	138
John Lavaroni	"	139
C. J. Strouse	"	140
Samuel Simmons	"	141
William Cunningham	"	142

ENGINE COMPANY No. 11.

Location—No. 1632 Fifteenth avenue South.

NAMES.	RANK.	NO. BADGE
C. H. Ferguson	Engineer.	144
James Hagan	Driver.	145
W. Barbotta	Fireman.	146
MEMBERS AT CALL.		
Charles Smith	Foreman.	143
Joseph Hoare	Assistant Foreman.	152
J. M. Rojas	Hoseman.	147
Peter Brady	"	148
C. F. McTiernan	"	149
William Farrell	"	150
Edward O'Sullivan	"	151
John Ford	"	153
Thomas McTiernan	"	154

ENGINE COMPANY No. 12.

Location—No. 101 Commercial street

NAMES.	RANK.	NO. BADGE.
Andrew Reid	Engineer.	156
William Hensley	Driver.	157
Frank Becker	Fireman.	158
MEMBERS AT CALL.		
Michael O'Brien	Foreman.	155
Chas. F. Smith	Assistant Foreman.	166
Thomas Lyons	Hoseman.	159
Robert Montgomery	"	160
Geo. Van Poon	"	161
Henry Behrmann	"	162
Patrick Heniker	"	163
Emile Gouvi	"	164
Edward Gillig	"	165
Charles F. Smith	"	166

ENGINE COMPANY No. 13.

Location—No. 1458 Valencia street.

NAMES.	RANK.	NO. BADGE.
J. F. McQuade.........	Engineer.	168
George McLaren...	Driver.	169
John Pendergast...	Fireman.	170
MEMBERS AT CALL.		
James Riley...	Foreman.	167
Jas. O'Connor...	Assistant Foreman.	176
John Scannel................................	Hoseman.	171
Thomas Rennilson	"	172
E. F. Cogger	"	173
Thomas Barry..	"	174
J. F. O'Donnell..	"	175
Albert McDonald...	"	177
George Faubel...	"	178

ENGINE COMPANY No. 14.

Location—No. 1017 McAllister street.

NAMES.	RANK.	NO. BADGE.
L. H. Barricks..................................	Engineer.	180
M. Hallihan...	Driver.	181
Bert Sorenson.......................................	Fireman.	182
MEMBERS AT CALL.		
William J. Kenealey....................................	Foreman.	179
Edward Richardson.....................................	Assistant Foreman.	190
David Levy..	Hoseman.	183
John Bowlan......................................	"	184
Hugh Powers........	"	185
Leo Castillo..	"	186
Reuben Levy..	"	187
Harry Tricou..	"	188
Albert Leaf....................................	"	189

ENGINE COMPANY No. 15.

Location—No. 2114 California street.

NAMES.	RANK.	NO. BADGE.
A. Imbrie	Engineer.	192
Frank Lerman.....	Driver.	193
Timothy O'Brien.....	Firemen.	194
MEMBERS AT CALL.		
Fred Whitaker.....	Foreman.	191
Geo. Brown.....	Assistant Foreman.	201
Thomas R. Walsh	Hoseman.	195
J. J. Moran.....	"	196
J. J. Mitchell.....	"	197
James Koopman.....	"	198
E. J. Moran.....	"	199
M. E. Wormuth.....	"	200
E. McIntyre.....	"	202

ENGINE COMPANY No. 16.

Location—No. 1009 Tennessee street.

NAMES.	RANK.	NO. BADGE.
Thomas McElroy.....	Engineer.	204
M. E. Gray	Driver.	205
B. F. Jones.....	Fireman.	206
MEMBERS AT CALL.		
C. J. Hogan.....	Foreman.	203
Martin Duddy.....	Assistant Foreman.	208
Geo. Symon	Hoseman.	207
William Moore.....	"	209
Hans Eskersen.....	"	210
Michael Cusack.....	"	211
Patrick O'Donnell.....	"	212
Daniel Toomey.....	"	213
Philip Moholy.....	"	214

ENGINE COMPANY No. 17.

Location—No. 34 Mint avenue.

NAMES.	RANK.	NO. BADGE.
William H. Kerrigan	Engineer.	216
Claude Brownell	Driver.	217
Frank McCluskey	Fireman.	218
MEMBERS AT CALL.		
John Doherty	Foreman.	215
J. J. Callen	Assistant Foreman.	225
James C. Crowley	Hoseman.	219
Wm. O'Farrell	"	220
Joseph Hayden	"	221
William Nicholson	"	222
James Dougherty	"	223
William Sawyer	"	224
Philip Deneby	"	226

ENGINE COMPANY No. 18.

Location—No. 317 Duncan street.

NAMES.	RANK.	NO. BADGE.
D. McLaughlin	Engineer.	228
Charles Thoney	Driver.	229
Charles Macdonald	Fireman.	230
MEMBERS AT CALL.		
William Holmes	Foreman.	227
Daniel Murphy	Assistant Foreman.	237
Joseph Teideman	Hoseman.	231
W. Wanderlich	"	232
Thomas Connors	"	233
Robert Strahle	"	234
Joseph Collins	"	235
John P. Reimers	"	236
Thomas P. Jones	"	238

ENGINE COMPANY No. 19.

Location—No. 1749 Market street.

NAMES.	RANK.	NO. BADGE.
S. P. Oppenheim	Engineer.	240
Daniel Farren	Driver.	241
Charles Bryan	Fireman.	242
MEMBERS AT CALL.		
H. F. Horn	Foreman.	239
John Matheson	Assistant Foreman.	244
H. Speckman	Hoseman.	243
John McCarthy	"	245
Wm. Smith.	"	246
Cornelius Kelleher	"	247
James Grace	"	248
J. O'Brien	"	249
Wm. Muenter	"	250

ENGINE COMPANY No. 20.

Location—No. 2117 Filbert street.

NAMES.	RANK.	NO. BADGE
Frank Crockett	Engineer.	252
Maurice Barrett	Driver.	253
James Tyrrell	Fireman.	254
MEMBERS AT CALL.		
Henry Schmidt	Foreman.	251
J. J. Kelly	Assistant Foreman.	260
Patrick Canty	Hoseman.	255
John Devlin	"	256
Richard Cosgrove	"	257
Myrtle Yohl	"	258
Percy J. Creede	"	259
John Gavin	"	261
John Fitzpatrick	"	262

ENGINE COMPANY No. 21.

Location—No. 1152 Oak street.

NAMES.	RANK.	NO. BADGE.
Henry Smith	Engineer.	264
Joseph Cully	Driver.	265
H. H. Smith	Fireman.	266
MEMBERS AT CALL.		
John Fay	Foreman.	263
Joseph Rodgers	Assistant Foreman.	274
Daniel Cooney	Hoseman.	267
Chas. F. O'Byrne	"	268
James Feeney	"	269
James Fitzgerald	"	270
J. F. Meacham	"	271
Henry Monseese	"	272
Charles Cochran	"	273

ENGINE COMPANY No. 22.

Location—No. 1819 Post street.

NAMES.	RANK.	NO. BADGE.
F. S. Hall	Engineer.	276
M. J. O'Connor	Driver.	277
James H. Stroud	Fireman.	278
MEMBERS AT CALL.		
John R. Mitchell	Foreman.	275
Thomas Collins	Assistant Foreman.	283
Robert Jones	Hoseman.	279
William Taylor	"	280
James Walsh	"	281
J. D. Sullivan	"	282
Theodore Yeazell	"	284
Edward McDermott	"	285
John McDonald	"	286

ENGINE COMPANY No. 23.

Location—No. 3022 Washington street.

NAMES.	RANK.	NO. BADGE.
Charles Hewitt	Engineer,	288
J. J. McCarthy	Driver.	289
Patrick Barry	Fireman.	290
MEMBERS AT CALL.		
James Layden	Foreman.	287
W. J. Shields	Assistant Foreman.	297
R. Oppenheim	Hoseman.	291
George McDonald	"	292
Gabriel Woods	"	293
A. W. Hallett	"	294
John Murphy	"	295
George Lawson	"	296
William F. Curran	"	298

ENGINE COMPANY No. 24.

Location—No. 449 Douglass street.

NAMES.	RANK.	NO. BADGE.
B. J. McShane	Engineer.	300
William O'Connor	Driver.	301
M. J. O'Connell	Fireman.	302
MEMBERS AT CALL.		
Edward Skelly	Foreman.	299
Eugene McCormick	Assistant Foreman	304
Joseph Lee	Hoseman.	303
Geo. W. Kamps	"	305
James Tuite	"	306
Fred J. Pope	"	307
William Mullaney	"	308
John S. Farley	"	309
Edward Toland	"	310

ENGINE COMPANY No. 25.

Location—No. 2547 Folsom street.

NAMES.	RANK.	NO. BADGE.
Joseph Finn	Engineer.	312
Malachi Norton	Driver.	313
John Hartford	Fireman.	314
MEMBERS AT CALL.		
James Radford	Foreman.	311
David Newell	Assistant Foreman.	316
Wm. Swanton	Hoseman.	315
Howard Marden	"	317
R. Jones	"	318
H. S. Morrison	"	319
Walter Nichols	"	320
P. F. Dugan	"	321
Thomas Pendergast	"	322

ENGINE COMPANY No. 26.

Location—No. 327 Second avenue.

NAMES.	RANK.	NO. BADGE.
John J. Murphy	Engineer.	324
Walter Lintott	Driver.	325
Henry Welch	Fireman.	326
MEMBERS AT CALL.		
James H. Dever	Foreman.	323
Michael Drury	Assistant Foreman.	331
John Owens	Hoseman.	327
Lewis Andrews	"	328
E. J. Sheddy	"	329
W. J. Wrin	"	330
Albert Ahlborn	"	332
M. Dougherty	"	333
Charles Harkins	"	334

5

ENGINE COMPANY No. 27.

Location—No. 621 Hermann street

NAMES.	RANK.	NO. BADGE.
J. T. Canavan	Engineer.	336
John T. Crummey	Driver.	337
W. F. Gallatin	Fireman.	338
MEMBERS AT CALL.		
R. H. Sawyer	Foreman.	335
Larry O'Neil	Assistant Foreman.	339
George F. Bunner	Hoseman.	340
John McGlynn	"	341
Edward O'Donnell	"	342
William Seiwert	"	343
John J. Nagle	"	345
James Walsh	"	346

ENGINE COMPANY No. 28.

Location—No. 301 Francisco street.

NAMES.	RANK.	NO. BADGE.
Joseph Pendergast	Engineer.	348
J. F. Sweeney	Driver.	349
John Maxwell	Fireman.	350
MEMBERS AT CALL.		
Fred Sayers	Foreman.	347
Jeremiah Sullivan	Assistant Foreman.	358
Thomas McGlynn	Hoseman.	351
John Arata	"	352
William King	"	353
William Jeffers	"	354
William Everson	"	355
C. S. Lawrence	"	356
J. Mitchell	"	357

ENGINE COMPANY No. 29

Location—No. 1305 Bryant street

NAMES.	RANK.	NO. BADGE
John Barry,	Engineer.	360
Thomas Hart	Driver.	361
Dennis Quinlan	Fireman.	362
MEMBERS AT CALL.		
William Byrne	Foreman.	359
Thomas J. Beans	Assistant Foreman.	370
Edward O'Malley	Hoseman.	363
John Murphy	"	364
Thomas Titus	"	365
Wallace Jamison	"	366
John Sweeney	"	367
James Flood	"	368
G. W. Hall	"	369

ENGINE COMPANY No. 30.

Location—No. 1737 Waller street.

NAMES.	RANK.	NO. BADGE.
M. Rodrigues	Engineer.	372
John Brophy	Driver.	373
Eugene Crummey	Fireman.	374
MEMBERS AT CALL.		
David R. Sewell	Foreman.	371
John Figuera	Assistant Foreman.	376
W. A. Cook	Hoseman.	375
Edward Kelleher	"	377
A. C. Goddard	"	378
George Lynch	"	379
Jeremiah Mahoney	"	380
John Enright	"	381
William Jordan	"	382

ENGINE COMPANY No. 31.

Location—No. 1236 Pacific street.

NAMES.	RANK.	NO. BADGE.
William T. Welch..	Engineer.	384
John Cahill..	Driver.	385
John Fitzsimmons...	Fireman.	386
MEMBERS AT CALL.		
Thomas Canty..	Foreman.	383
Edward McConigle...	Assistant Foreman.	387
John O'Brien...	Hoseman.	388
M. J. O'Brien..	"	389
Martin Burns...	"	390
Joseph F. Shaughnessy....................................	"	391
James Mathews...	"	392
Charles O'Malley...	"	393
James Walsh...	"	394

*ENGINE COMPANY No. 32.

Location—Holly Park and West Avenue.

NAMES.	RANK.	NO. BADGE.
William Caseholt	Engineer.	396
John Blythe..	Driver.	397
William Murphy...	Fireman.	398
MEMBERS AT CALL.		
Eugene O'Connor..	Foreman.	395
John R. Thompson	Assistant Foreman.	399
James J. Fay...	Hoseman.	400
J. J. McCarthy...	"	401
James Bohan...	"	402
Michael O'Neil...	"	403
L. A. Smith..	"	404
David Casey..	"	405
George W. Lahnsen..	"	406

ENGINE COMPANY No. 33.

Location—No. 117 Broad street.

NAMES.	RANK.	NO. BADGE.
William Heaney	Engineer.	408
Jerry McNamara	Driver.	409
William Blackmore	Fireman.	410
MEMBERS AT CALL.		
R. T. Brown	Foreman.	407
John Caully	Assistant Foreman.	414
Frank Josephs	Hoseman.	411
John Cannon	"	412
George Clancy	"	413
John Casserly	"	415
Thomas Johnson	"	416
Eugene E. Casserly	"	417
John McLaughlin	"	418

ENGINE COMPANY No. 34.

Location—No. 1119 Ellis street.

NAMES.	RANK.	NO. BADGE.
Louis Kiehl	Engineer.	558
Samuel Nelson	Driver.	559
James Buckley	Fireman.	560
MEMBERS AT CALL.		
Henry Mitchell	Foreman.	557
George Farley	Assistant Foreman.	561
William Hanten	Hoseman.	562
Daniel E. Twomey	"	563
Harry Newman	"	564
Chas. A. Heineman	"	565
W. P. Conlin	"	566
Frank Quinn	"	567
Anthony Phelan	"	568

TRUCK COMPANY No. 1.

Location—No. 22 O'Farrell street.

NAMES.	RANK.	NO. BADGE.
C. Connell ..	Driver.	420
George Carew	Tillerman.	421
MEMBERS AT CALL.		
E. Crowe	Foreman.	419
Frank Nichols	Assistant Foreman.	422
Hugh Quinn	Truckman.	423
Joseph Wolf	"	424
Joseph Brown	"	425
Geo. T. Logan	"	426
Daniel Donovan	"	427
Thomas Gallagher	"	428
Robert H. Woods	"	429
W. F. Tracey	"	430
John J. Quinn	"	431
Brown P. Haugen	"	432
W. A. St. Amant	"	433

TRUCK COMPANY No. 2.

Location—No. 627 Broadway

NAMES.	RANK	NO. BADGE.
J. S. Brant	Driver.	435
A. Florance	Tillerman,	436
MEMBERS AT CALL.		
John Dryer	Foreman.	434
Joseph Capelli	Assistant Foreman.	447
Frank Kruse	Truckman.	437
John Leahy	"	438
J. F. Dooley	"	439
H. Donnadeau	"	440
John Crosby	"	441
Rinaldo Cuneo	"	442
Joseph Burke	"	443
Harry Wilson	"	444
Henry Mulligan	"	445
Joseph Dunn	"	446
Frank Cummings	"	448

TRUCK COMPANY No. 3.

Location—No. 1749 Market street.

NAMES.	RANK.	NO. BADGE.
Michael Hannan........	Driver.	450
Joseph Burnett..	Tillerman.	451
MEMBERS AT CALL.		
William Schultz	Foreman.	449
E. Kehoe..	Assistant Foreman.	462
George Clancey...	Truckman	452
A. Jensen	"	453
Joseph Vincent...	"	454
C. W. Heggum...	"	455
Mark Bearwald............................	"	456
John J. Kenney...	"	457
John Manion	"	458
M. Fitzhenry...	"	459
James Driscoll....................................	"	460
Earnest Cameron	"	461
William Frodsham..	"	463

TRUCK COMPANY No. 4.

Location—No. 1648 Pacific avenue.

NAMES.	RANK.	NO. BADGE.
Maurice Higgins...........	Driver.	465
Frank Carew......................................	Tillerman.	466
MEMBERS AT CALL.		
J. W. Kentzel	Foreman.	464
J. E. Eckelmann	Assistant Foreman.	467
T. B. Kentzel...	Truckman.	468
W. H. Kelly........	"	469
Thomas Timmons..	"	470
George Donald..........	"	471
Joseph Corwell..	"	472
H. T. Heffernan	"	473
George Davis..	"	474
E. F. Murray..	"	475
Henry O'Neil..	"	476
Patrick Hogan...	"	477
E. P. Brennan...	"	478

TRUCK COMPANY No. 5.

Location—No. 1819 Post street.

NAMES.	RANK.	NO. BADGE.
Charles Mulloy......................................	Driver	480
William F. Otto....................................	Tillerman.	481
MEMBERS AT CALL.		
Edward Kingsley....................................	Foreman.	479
Wm. Serens..	Assistant Foreman.	484
R. P. Jackman.....................................	Truckman	482
Matthew Farley.....................................	"	483
T. J. Harrington...................................	"	485
Frank Koopman.....................................	"	486
R. S. Chapman.....................................	"	487
Joseph Morse......................................	"	488
R. Powers...	"	489
Henry McMahon.....................................	"	490
....	"	491
J. H. O'Brien......................................	"	492
John Flynn...	"	493

TRUCK COMPANY No. 6.

Location—No. 1152 Oak street.

NAMES.	RANK.	NO. BADGE.
John P. Hayden....................................	Driver.	495
James Cumiskey....................................	Tillerman.	496
MEMBERS AT CALL.		
W. E. Kelly.......................................	Foreman.	494
Walter Boynton....................................	Assistant Foreman.	499
George M. Boyson..................................	Truckman.	497
M. Flannigan......................................	"	498
H. H. Casey.......................................	"	500
Joseph Aspden.....................................	"	501
J. Grote..	"	502
James Franks......................................	"	503
Gustave Hain......................................	"	504
Alexander George..................................	"	505
Joseph McNamara...................................	"	506
David Wright......................................	"	507
James A. Riley....................................	"	508

TRUCK COMPANY No. 7.

Location—No. 3050 Seventeenth street.

NAMES.	RANK.	NO. BADGE.
Eugene Sheridan..	Driver.	510
Julius de Meyer...	Tillerman.	511
MEMBERS AT CALL.		
William Carew..	Foreman.	509
William J. Bannan	Assistant Foreman.	514
Charles Maguire	Truckman.	512
Frank Johnson............................	"	513
Fred Woods	"	515
James J. O'Connor..	"	516
F. A. Ellenberg...........	"	517
Andrew Chesney.............	"	518
Henry Sullivan	"	519
John Pyne..	"	520
Michael Wright...............................	"	521
William O'Connor...	"	522
Thomas F. Fitzpatrick........................	"	523

CHEMICAL ENGINE COMPANY No. 1.

Location—No. 144 Second street.

NAMES.	RANK.	NO. BADGE.
Thomas Mahon...	Engineer.	524
Richard J. Allen...	Driver.	525
Peter Burke..	Fireman.	526
William Matheson......	Steward.	527

CHEMICAL ENGINE COMPANY No. 2.

Location—No. 1318 Tenth Avenue.

NAMES.	RANK.	NO. BADGE
	Engineer.	528
Paul Demartini..	Driver.	529
Martin Spellman	Fireman.	530
William Crawhall...	Steward.	531

CHEMICAL ENGINE COMPANY No. 3.

Location—No. 112 Jackson street.

NAMES.	RANK.	NO. BADGE.
Thomas Murphy	Engineer.	532
William Shackleton	Driver.	533
T. J. Kelly	Fireman.	534
James Minigan	Steward.	535

CHEMICAL ENGINE COMPANY No. 4.

Location—No. 451 McAllister street.

NAMES.	RANK.	NO. BADGE.
Isadore Gurmendez	Engineer.	536
Thomas McGovern	Driver.	537
James Britt	Fireman.	538
Edward King	Steward.	539

CHEMICAL ENGINE COMPANY No. 5.

Location—No. 627 Broadway.

NAMES.	RANK.	NO. BADGE.
William Gallatin	Engineer.	540
William Newman	Driver.	541
John F. Riley	Fireman.	542
Julius Phillips	Steward.	543

CHEMICAL ENGINE COMPANY No. 6.

Location—No. 311 Sixth street.

NAMES.	RANK.	NO BADGE.
James Conniff	Engineer.	544
William Hart	Driver.	545
James Laudtbum	Fireman.	546
Frank Sullivan	Steward.	547

CHEMICAL ENGINE COMPANY No. 7.

Locatton—No. 3050 Seventeenth street.

NAMES.	RANK.	NO. BADGE.
George Bailey	Engineer.	548
Howard Holmes.	Driver.	549
George Ewing	Fireman.	550
J. D. Devine	Steward.	551

WATER TOWER COMPANY No. 1.

Location—No. 108 New Montgomery street.

NAMES.	RANK.	NO. BADGE.
Peter Wralty	Engineer.	552
Edward J. Shaughnessy	Driver.	553
John Riley	Fireman.	554

MONITOR BATTERY No. 1.

Location—No. 516 Bryant street.

NAME.	RANK.	NO. BADGE.
Christopher Windrow	Driver.	555

MONITOR BATTERY No. 2.

Location—No. 22 O'Farrell street.

NAME.	RANK.	NO. BADGE.
Joseph Wales	Driver.	556

RELIEF ENGINE COMPANIES.

DESIGNATED AS FIFTH ALARM COMPANIES.

RELIEF ENGINE COMPANY No. 1.

Headquarters—Corporation Yard No. 2.

NAME.	RANK.
John Riley	Foreman.
E. E. McKittrick	Engineer.
John Sheehan	Fireman.
Arthur Price	Hoseman.
Henry H. Gorter	"

RELIEF ENGINE COMPANY No. 2.

Headquarters—Engine House No. 3.

NAME.	RANK.
Walter Cline	Foreman.
J. J. Conlon	Engineer.
John Hurley	Fireman.
James Hanley	Hoseman.
J. H. Smith	"
William Hart	"
Luke Curry	"

RELIEF ENGINE COMPANY No. 3.

Headquarters—Engine House No. 15.

NAME.	RANK.
Chas. Healy	Foreman.
William Waters	Engineer.
William Brown	Fireman.
D. McKibben	Hoseman.
J. H. Browning	"
James Byrnes	"
Joseph Harrington	"

RELIEF ENGINE COMPANY No. 4.

Headquarters—Waller Street Storehouse.

NAME.	RANK.
Isador Gurmendez	Foreman.
John McCluskey	Engineer.
Samuel Rainey	Fireman.
D. Quinlan	Hoseman.
Thomas McLaughlin	"
Walter Molloy	"
Thomas Bulger	"

RELIEF ENGINE COMPANY No. 5.

Headquarters—Department Stables.

NAME.	RANK.
Henry Rice	Foreman.
Frank Lester	Engineer
Edward Payne	Fireman.
Philip Brady	Hoseman
John Kearney	"
Patrick Kane	"

LOCATION OF DEPARTMENT WORKSHOPS, ETC.

BUILDINGS.	LOCATION.
Corporation Yard No. 1	No. 50 Sacramento street.
Corporation Yard No. 1	No. 307 Francisco street.
Plumbing Shop	No. 1229 Bryant street.
Carpenter Shop	No. 742 13th street.
Department Stables	No. 534 Tenth street.

.Report of Superintendent

of the

Fire Alarm and Police Telegraph.

———

San Francisco, July 1, 1899.

To the Honorable the Board of Supervisors
Of the City and County of San Francisco—

Gentlemen: I have the honor to submit herewith the Thirty-fourth Annual Report of the Fire Alarm and Police Telegraph, for the fiscal year ending June 20, 1899.

WM. R. HEWITT,
Superintendent F. A. & P. T.

———

EXTENSIONS AND IMPROVEMENTS.

During the past year this department received a total of 828 alarms, of which there were 492 first, 11 second, 4 third, 1 fourth and 320 still alarms.

The total number of police calls recorded is 97,427.

There are in operation 267 gongs and tappers, 531 miles of wire, 2,282 cells of battery, 278 fire boxes and 200 police boxes, 43 engine house equipments, and 5 central police systems.

The circuits were extended to Ocean View, and considerable reconstruction and extensions were made to the circuits of the City, requiring about 257 poles and 70 miles of wire.

The poles and boxes were painted, 9 new fire boxes were erected during the year, the location of 9 fire boxes changed, 14 boxes rebuilt, 62 fire boxes and 31 police boxes were taken down, repaired at shop and reset, 31 new character wheels were made, the locks of 75 fire boxes polished and trapped, the numbers of 3 fire boxes changed, and 9 fire boxes changed to keyless door boxes; 7 boxes were changed from one signal circuit to another signal circuit.

In all new Fire Department houses, as well as those extensively repaired, was placed an iron armored conduit system for electric lighting and two houses were connected up for lighting circuits. The houses were also wired for complete alarm systems and equipped with new sounding boards on the "silent" system.

The Repair Shop of this department is now fully equipped and prepared to attend to all repair jobs, besides turning out new work in the shape of new fire and police boxes and engine house and police station equipments.

Additional shop room was secured by fitting up two adjoining rooms in the City Hall basement.

In one room will be finished and assembled all new engine house equipments, and the other has been fitted up as a laboratory for electrical purposes, where we are now prepared to make any of the elaborate tests necessary in underground cable and inspection work.

Thirty new fire boxes complete and fifteen engine house oak sounding boards, including the equipment of tapper relay bells, registers, take-up reels, ground test switches and joker bell outfits, were made.

About 600 emergency repair jobs were attended to during the year.

We are now wiring all engine houses for the "silent" alarm system and electric lights, placing our wires underground, and exercising a general inspection and supervision of all electric wiring in and on buildings and streets in the City and County.

An appropriation of $20,000 was allowed for placing the wires underground.

The factory district east of Third and south of Market street was mapped out and provision made for permanent service, such as will meet the demands of the future.

It was estimated that, in addition to the conduits of the Pacific Telephone and Telegraph Company, which the City is privileged to use, there would be required to cover the district, 20,000 feet main conduit, 20,000 feet lateral conduit, 39 manholes, 41 boxes, 45,000 feet of cable, 600,000 feet of conductor.

The conduit is of 2½-inch steel pipe for main conduit, and 1¼-inch pipe for lateral, specially reamed and straightened, and was given two coats of extra heavy asphalt by a special process, so that the coat was soft, elastic and tough enough to withstand any ordinary abrasion, and yet so hard as not to become tacky, and finally laid with a concrete jacket at joints.

Owing to the delay in finally fixing the appropriation, work was not begun until the latter part of 1895.

The vacant Fire Department lot on Sixteenth street, between Folsom and Harrison streets, was obtained for the use of this department, and storehouses for conduit and miscellaneous supplies, and a plant for preparing conduit, were erected.

The trench work was started on April 4th, at Spear and Folsom streets, and practically finished June 30, 1899.

There now remains to be done the work of drawing in the cables, and the erection of new fire boxes.

A map of the City and County showing the location of all boxes connected to the underground system and of the municipal buildings connected to this service, was made on a scale of 400 feet to 1 inch, laid out on a mat of 1-inch sugar pine boards, 10 feet high and 9 feet 6 inches wide, and is practically without error when compared with the United States survey.

At the request of the Merchants' Association, an Order was prepared by this office for the placing of electric wires underground within the period of three years, and was passed by your Honorable Board August 14, 1899.

Blue print maps were made of the underground districts and distributed to the various companies owning and controlling wires in this City and County.

All electric wiring in buildings being repaired and in the course of construction has been regularly inspected by this department, in order that electric wiring may be brought up to the proper standard and the risk of fires from electric wires cut down to a minimum.

At the Baldwin Hotel fire the lives of many people were endangered because of the lights being suddenly extinguished, due to the blowing of the main fuses.

To overcome the possibility of a repetition of this danger, I have ordered that an emergency circuit be placed in all hotels, theaters, and other public buildings.

In the Grand Opera House this circuit is so arranged that the house may be left in entire darkness with the exception of single lights over exits and in passage ways, controlled by a switch near the main entrance and next to the street service, accessible at all times to firemen and police.

These circuits are never used except for tests and emergencies, and are not a part of the common lighting service of the house.

This is about the only large city in the country that has not an Order regulating the installation of electric wires, complying with the rules and regulations of the National Board of Underwriters.

I would recommend that an Order be passed authorizing this department to issue certificates under these rules without cost to the property owner, certifying to the efficiency of the work done.

The frequent requests made by architects, owners and contractors for a written report of the inspection, makes the necessity of such an Order almost imperative.

The increasing demand on the services of this department renders the present appropriation insufficient for its requirements.

Aside from the natural growth of the business of this office, due to an increase in population, which means the protection of new territory as well as the maintenance of a possibly better service in the business sections, this department has increased responsibilities and burdens because of the general application of electricity during the past ten years for lighting, power, railways, telephone and telegraph systems.

At present all of these systems are so closely interwoven with the municipal wires that a change in one affects all, compelling a constant demand for the services of our linemen, such as could not be contemplated when the appropriation was fixed for this department, and there follows increased expense for labor in the maintenance of the system.

Provision should be made in the next appropriation for 300 new fire boxes, the placing of wires under ground under your Order No. 214 (New Series), a direct telephone system connecting all department stations with this office, and a new office, the present quarters not permitting an increase in the circuits, which are now dangerously overloaded and of extreme length.

One hundred and twenty-eight dollars received from house movers was turned into the Treasury.

EXPENDITURES FIRE ALARM AND POLICE TELEGRAPH FOR FISCAL YEAR 1898-99.

MONTH.	Totals	Labor	Time	Horse Expenses	Miscellaneous	Paints and Oils	Stationery and Printing	Machinery	Tools and Hardware	Boxes and Instruments	Shop Supplies	Line Material	Battery Material
1898—July	$3,168 26	$2,191 95	$25 00	$425 00	$28 65	$20 52		$12 50	$35 71	$329 90	$25 70	$22 77	$40 96
August	2,941 04	2,441 60	25 00	142 00	48 60	50 10	$5 00		40 16		106 46	07 43	8 09
September	4,168 52	2,736 65	25 00	266 50	139 29	103 38	3 25	107 27	62 25	146 80	30 01	495 00	63 12
October	5,789 33	2,940 97	25 00	255 85	292 08	29 92	12 85	530 52	312 37	13 79	23 23	1,302 90	44 55
November	5,310 04	3,249 00	25 00	164 40	405 41	713 60	49 00	68 36	116 07	284 16	70 91	113 47	50 00
December	5,088 31	3,330 0·	25 00	219 60	51 61	65	30 85		161 38	2 12	57 48	1,008 64	201 93
1899—January	6,718 88	3,098 6·	25 00	106 00	110 44	29 10	30 25	2 50	284 31	25 84	58 61	2,289 08	19 10
February	7,429 38	4,318 00	25 00	215 80	117 70	57 40	3 45		353 02	472 57	129 73	1,646 43	89 53
March	7,206 07	5,138 40	25 00	309 20	404 60	273 35	5 25	78	241 64	126 32	73 88	599 89	7 76
April	7,073 43	5,183 50	25 00	210 40	232 66	137 29	22 95		164 94	19 23	30 75	947 96	98 80
May	6,598 82	5,346 55	25 00	205 50	28 23	10 80	16 13	1 19	309 51	68	24 13	543 60	87 50
June	6,603 82	5,229 50	25 00	198 00	36 62	63 61	2 05		156 52	15 00	125 05	678 20	74 27
Totals	$68,095 96	$45,704 77	$300 00	$2,778 94	$1,895 95	$1,405 78	$190 03	$729 12	$2,209 08	$1,436 41	$755 94	$9,714 67	$795 26

Total appropriations..$68,100 00
Total expenditures......... .... 68,095 95

Surplus................................. .... $4 05

Returned to General Fund —

Surplus.. $4 05
Housemover 128 00

Total......... .. .. $132 05

Aside from the regular appropriation allowed, a special appropriation of $8,227.30 was made for the payment of 45,000 feet of cable of various sizes and carrying 600,000 feet of conductor.

This payment could have been made from the regular appropriation of $68,100, but, owing to a delay in the delivery of the cable by the manufacturers, due to a rush of work caused by the Government war orders, the money was expended for other purposes, principally for underground labor.

www.ingramcontent.com/pod-product-compliance
Lightning Source LLC
Chambersburg PA
CBHW030006030726
47499CB00008B/2924